THE ADVENTURES OF TIMMY TINT & LYTHARI

RIKHIA GUHA

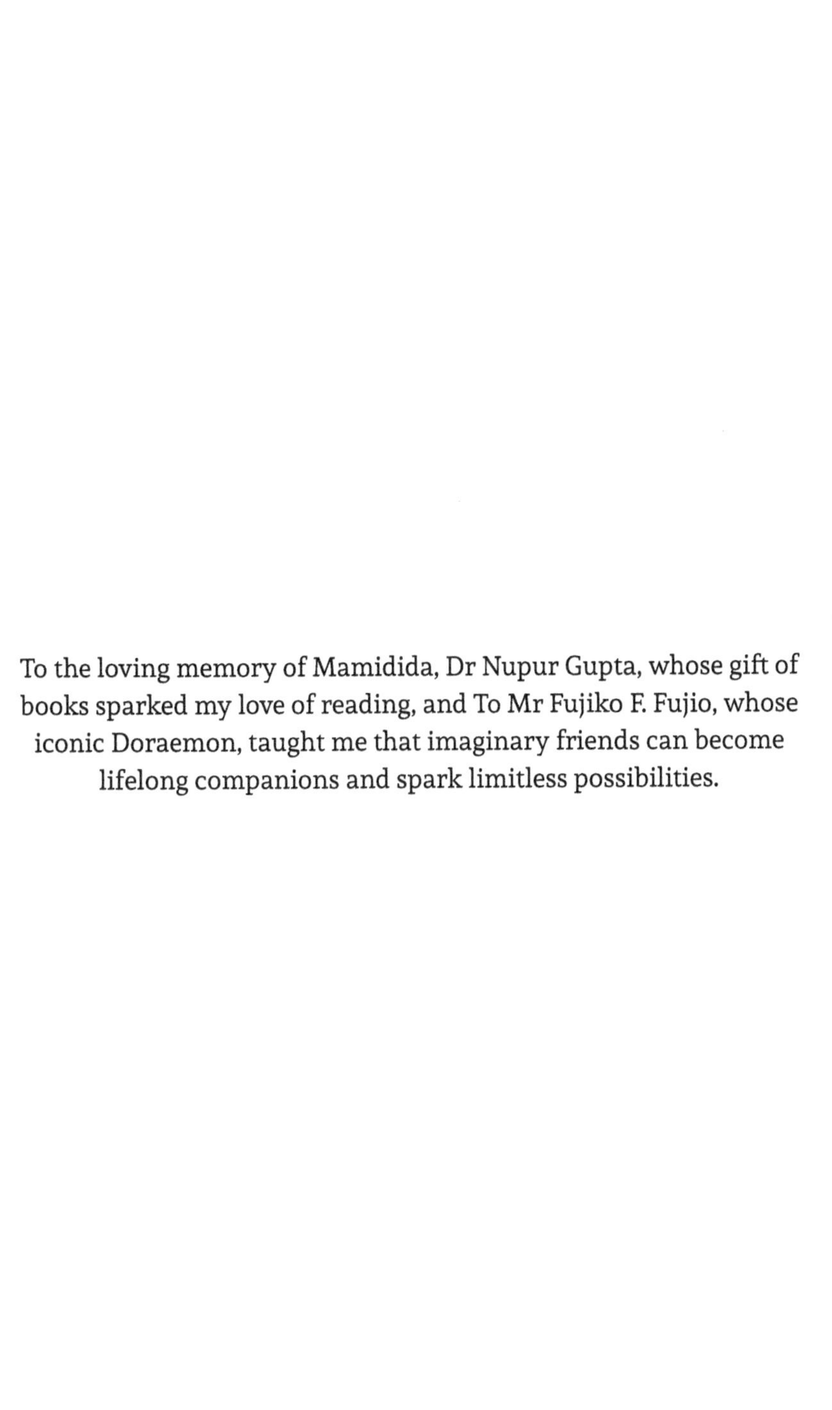

To the loving memory of Mamidida, Dr Nupur Gupta, whose gift of books sparked my love of reading, and To Mr Fujiko F. Fujio, whose iconic Doraemon, taught me that imaginary friends can become lifelong companions and spark limitless possibilities.

Contents

Contents

Acknowledgements

I'm grateful to Ms Asmita Baidya for her meticulous editing and insightful suggestions. Thank you for putting so much effort and heart into this work and loving it like your own. Your inputs were beyond valuable.

Digital Illustrations by first time illustrator, Simi Biswas. Thank you for visually enhancing this story.

Hugs to my dear friend, Deepanwita Paul for the beautiful original art work on cover, the 1st thing that catches an eye and brings in curiosity towards the subject, words wouldn't be enough to thank you. You can find more of her artwork on Instagram @deepanwita.art. From sharing a bench and our Tiffin at school to sharing space on this 'heart work', we are a team!

Special thanks to my parents for instilling the love for reading and writing in me pretty early in life.

And to my husband, whose relentless encouragement (even when annoyingly persistent!) helped this 'hyperactive brain lazy body' author stay focused. Your post-edit communication skills saved me from social anxiety.

Foreword

This is a story of a pre-teen boy who is learning how to navigate life. Aided by his Spirit guide Lythari, he goes on adventures in places far far away; or at times to those places which never even exist.

Timmy discovers in a safe environment that bad things and challenges do happen to everyone and finally "the Knight in shinning armour" does come to the rescue. Only that, the Knight emerges from within, he's always been there waiting to be found.

With the turn of every page, I found a kindered spirit in Timmy. Riddled with questions that has been hammering my teenage mind and slowly discovering that life will not always be so difficult and so insanely gruesome at every turn. It does get better, calmer and there are far brighter days than my teenage self would have ever imagined !!

As an avid reader of Fairy tales who always dreams in bright luminous colours sprinkled with confetti and sparkles !! This was an absolute treat for me and I'm overwhelmed by the Honour of being the First reader of this fascinating script !!

-- Indira Mitra

If you don't at least try, you will never change.
~Doraemon

Prologue

The Dream-weaver

In realms beyond mortal comprehension, a celestial tapestry weaves together the threads of fate, connecting lives across dimensions. Among these threads, a special bond was forged – a bond between a young boy and a majestic creature born from the essence of stars.

In a world where magic whispers secrets to those who listen, there unfolded a prophecy:

A heart once broken shall find solace,
A spirit once lost shall find guidance.
Through love and sacrifice, a bridge shall form.
Between worlds, a guardian shall emerge.

In a small town nestled between rolling hills and sun-kissed skies, a family's story began – the story of love, loss, and the transformative power of connection.

This is the tale of Timmy, a young boy destined to discover the magic within himself, and Lythari, the Guardian who would change his life forever.

....

Preface

Every night, 10-year-old Timmy eagerly awaited bedtime. He was not exactly fond of sleeping, but he slept nevertheless to embark on magical adventures in his dreams. As soon as his parents tucked him in, he'd snuggle under the blankets, close his eyes, and drift into a world of wonder. It's been more than 3 years of his nocturnal quests and still every night it felt as exciting and curious.

In his dreams, a magnificent creature named Lythari welcomed him. With iridescent wings, golden paws, and a shimmering snow-white fur coat, Lythari would sweep Timmy away to enchanted forests, where ancient trees whispered secrets and fireflies danced like tiny lanterns.

Each night, Lythari presented Timmy with a new quest. Along with his help, Timmy battled mischievous sprites, solved ancient riddles, and discovered hidden treasures. His imagination soared as he explored mystical realms, his courage and wit growing with each triumph.

By day, Timmy struggled to contain his excitement.

He'd burst into school, eager to share his nocturnal exploits with his friends.

"Last night, Lythari and I outran a pack of shadow wolves!" Or "Last night, Lythari and I discovered a hidden city within a hollow tree!"

But the boys rolled their eyes at his stories, mocking him. "You're just making it all up, Timmy!" they'd say.

Mrs Johnson, their Social Science teacher, would give him a kind smile and guide the conversation back to lessons.

At home, Mr and Mrs Tint were worried sick.

"Is he lonely?" Mrs Tint would ask her husband. "Maybe he's creating this fantasy world to cope?"

"We'll keep an eye on him, but I think we're worrying for nothing after all. Perhaps he's just- *creative*," Mr Tint reassured her.

One evening, as they put their son to bed and kissed him good night, Mrs Tint heard him whisper to her, "Mummy, Lythari's waiting for me."

She smiled. The innocent spark in his eyes was enough to fill a mother's heart. "Have a wonderful adventure, sweetie" she said softly, and put out the night lamp.

That night, Lythari took Timmy to a lake of shimmering moonstones. They sailed across its tranquil waters in a ship made of corals, guided by a constellation of glowing fish. Timmy's heart swelled with joy, knowing this magical world was only his to uncover.

The next morning at school, Timmy's enthusiasm overflowed. Pouring his dream out onto his notebook, he drew pictures of Lythari and the moonstone lake where he'd spotted fish with bodies of glitter.

The boys next to him looked at each other and snickered, but Miss Lawrence, their Art teacher, noticed the intricate details and vibrant colours in the drawing.

Once the bell rang and the class was over, she approached Timmy. "Your stories may not seem real to your friends, but your creativity is remarkable. I love your stories and I was thinking, would you like to illustrate the school magazine, Timmy? I'll talk to the Art faculty then."

At this, Timmy's cheeks turned red and he couldn't hold back his smile.

He'd always liked Miss Lawrence – unlike the others in his class, she was always nice and sweet to him – and he was too excited to miss this opportunity.

"Yes Miss! I'd love to" he exclaimed. He gave himself an imaginative pat on the back, having finally achieved a creative outlet for all his 'unbelievable' adventures with Lythari.

As the days went by, Timmy's tales continued to unfold, both in his dreams and in the school book. Lythari remained his one true companion, guiding him through enchanted realms. People around him didn't understand any of it and dismissed his stories as make-believe, but Timmy knew they were real. They were real in his mind, where his imagination knew no bounds.

Years passed. Timmy became a renowned author, weaving tales of Lythari and his fantastical quests with him. Children worldwide devoured his books, and critics praised his boundless creativity. At book-signing sessions, fans would ask, "Where do you get such marvellous ideas from, Mr Tint?" Timmy simply smiled. "From my dreams" he'd say, "And my magical friend, Lythari."

ONE

THE QUEST FOR THE GOLDEN ACORN

As Timmy drifted off to sleep, Lythari, as usual, awaited him in the dream realm. The majestic creature's wings, glistening like stardust, illuminated the moonlit forest.

"Tonight, young adventurer, we embark on a perilous quest" Lythari announced, his voice like gentle thunder. "The ancient Tree of Wisdom has lost its Golden Acorn, the source of its magical powers. We must retrieve it from the clutches of Puck, the mischievous forest sprite."

Timmy's heart raced with excitement. "I'm ready, Lythari. Let's fly!"

Together, they soared through the enchanted forest, navigating paths lined with glittering fireflies and silver-leaved trees. The air smelt of the sweet scent of blooming wildflowers. They crossed the Sparkling Stream where the fish swam in synchronized patterns, their scales shining in the sun like diamonds.

Timmy marvelled, "Lythari, look! The fish are dancing!" Lythari chuckled. "The forest often performs for us, Timmy. We're its honoured guests."

They entered the realm of the Forgotten Gardens, where vines grew wrapped around ancient statues, and flowers bloomed in every colour of the rainbow. Puck's playful laughter echoed through the gardens.

"Ah, Puck is hiding in his tree house," Lythari whispered, pointing to a twisted tree with prisms dangling from its branches. "We must be cautious, Timmy. His tricks and illusions can confuse even the wisest of minds."

As they approached the tree house, Puck appeared. A small sylph with his wings fluttering like a butterfly, he declared, "Welcome, Lythari and young Timmy! I've been expecting you. You can try as much as you want, but you'll never get to claim the Golden Acorn. It's hidden within my labyrinth of reflections." He gave out a mirthful laughter.

Timmy stood tall. "We'll solve your labyrinth, Puck! We're not afraid" he said confidently.

Puck grinned mischievously. "Yeah, we'll see about that. Enter, *brave adventurers!*" he mocked.

As they entered Puck's labyrinth, Timmy spotted a number of mirrors. Looking closely, he realised that these mirrors reflected his deepest fears and desires.

The first mirror showed Timmy failing in school, his grades plummeting, and his parents disappointed. Timmy's heart sank; he hesitated.

But Lythari's gentle voice calmed him, "Timmy, this is not your reality. Your worth extends beyond your grades."

Timmy took a deep breath and stepped forward.

The next mirror revealed Timmy's fear of losing his parents. He saw himself alone, scared and crying. Tears welled up in his eyes.

But again, Lythari was there to offer words of comfort, "Your parents love you, Timmy, you know that. They'll always be there for you. Death is what comes with life, but even in death, your parents will remain by you, if you believe it in your heart."

Timmy's determination grew. "You're right, Lythari. I won't let my fears get the better of me."

As they ventured deeper, Timmy saw another mirror that reflected his desire for acceptance. He saw his classmates mocking him and excluding him from games. All those times when they'd laughed at the stories of his adventures, flashed before his eyes. He lowered his head with self-pity and embarrassment.

Lythari saw his friend losing will as Timmy stopped on his track and looked back with tearful eyes. The Guardian stepped forward, put one of his wings on Timmy's shoulder, and reminded him, "True friends accept you for who you are, dear friend.

Like I do. You don't need to seek your validation from others. You validate yourself."

At this, Timmy squared his shoulders. "Yes! Yes Lythari, I am worthy of friendship. I have a friend like you after all." Lythari smiled. The two of them moved forward.

Puck's illusions intensified, as the tiny trickster attempted to confuse them. Mirrors distorted their reflections, making it seem like Lythari was leading Timmy astray. "Is this the right path? Are you sure, Lythari?" Timmy asked, uncertain. Lythari's wisdom guided him, "Remember, these mirrors are but reflecting devices meant to deceive you. What matters is the reflection of your soul. Look within yourself, and you'll know your truth."

Timmy closed his eyes and aimed all his focus onto his heart. He thought about his love for Lythari, and immediately felt his nerves cool as he remembered how much he trusted his guidance. When he opened his eyes, the mirrors were all clear.

"It is the real path! Puck's trying to trick me by telling me otherwise. But I won't be fooled so easily."

Lythari nodded, smiling, "Your heart guides us, young one."

Finally, they reached the centre of the labyrinth, where the Golden Acorn shone brightly. Puck attempted to confuse them with a final, dazzling illusion – a mirror reflecting Timmy's deepest desire: becoming a hero.

Lythari noticed a tinge of uncertainty in the little boy's eyes. Softly, the angel said, "Timmy, you know he is playing with us. This is not your truth. Your worth isn't measured by grand heroic acts. Heroism also means having the courage to move forward despite life's obstacles. You shouldn't let the latter cloud your judgement."

Timmy's mind filled with conviction, "I know who I am. I am brave, I am kind, and yes, I am worthy!"

As soon as he said these words, he felt a jolt of energy pass through his body. With one final glance at Lythari, Timmy ran to the point where the magical acorn was placed, a colourful whirlwind of stardust and bright green light fought against his tiny hands that tried to grab the acorn, the mighty roots of the trees curled and held him at his ankles, trying to trip him over, the mischievous laughter of Puck reverberated through the ancient branches and hanging roots, Timmy was determined, no wind was strong enough to keep him away, like a magnetic connection he felt his hand fly towards the gleaming pulsing light that emanated from the golden acorn and in no time it was in his grip, the roots loosened around his ankles no longer fighting the tiny adventurer, the green stardust mixed whirlwind disappeared with a final whiff and sigh. Timmy felt grounded again , he sighed in relief and held the Golden Acorn up for his friend to see. That was the widest he had seen the majestic Angel smile.

As they returned the Golden Acorn to the Tree of Wisdom, its energy was restored. Its ancient voice whispered, "Well done, brave adventurer. Your heart's wisdom and courage have illuminated the forest."

When Timmy woke the next morning, he found that the memory of the quest still lingered in his mind. He knew he'd never forget it, and that the things he learned in this one dream will inspire him for the rest of his life.

TWO

THE PRINCIPAL'S OFFICE

The next morning, Timmy arrived at school wearing his heart on his sleeve. He was still basking in the thrill of his dream adventure. Spotting his friends Emma, Max and Olivia chatting by the lockers, he ran to them to pour it all out.

"Guys! You won't believe what happened last night!" he exclaimed, launching into a vivid retelling of his journey through the labyrinth.

The whole time Timmy narrated his quest, his friends did not say a word. They listened with rapt attention, and occasionally looked at each other in awe and bewilderment. But once he finished his account and looked at them eagerly, raised an eyebrow, "Okay Timmy that was quite a story."

Max snickered. "Yeah right. You expect us to believe you flew with an Angel. What's his name again? *Lie-tari*?" They all burst into laughter.

Olivia chimed in, "Oh Timmy, you're always making stuff up. We're not buying it this time."

Emma, his best friend, came to his rescue. Although she didn't believe Timmy's story entirely, she did not like the way everyone was attacking him. "Alright guys, that's it. I think we should leave now, or we'll be late for class. Timmy, you're joining us, right?"

Timmy nodded. "You guys go ahead. I need to arrange a few things in my locker. I'll join you in class." Emma gave him a supportive smile, and the three of them walked away.

Timmy was glad that Emma had stood up for him. But he saw a few others in the corridor staring at him and laughing amongst them. Maybe they had overheard the conversation. It didn't matter, since Timmy's enthusiasm had already faltered. His cheeks burned with shame and regret, regret of thinking he could ever share his stories with someone. He turned around, and thought of going to his class and sitting alone at his desk. Or maybe he could sit beside Emma, like always. After all, she was the only person at school who did not make him feel lesser. "Yes, I'll do that" he whispered to himself, and turned around to go to class.

Just then, a group of boys from the school's football team, led by their star quarterback, Jake, walked past the corridor. But on seeing everyone looking at Timmy and snickering, they approached him. "Hey Timmy! Still spinning tales, are you?" Jake sneered.

One of the boys pulled Timmy's backpack down from his shoulders and kicked it, sending books and pens scattering.

"Liar!" another boy shouted.

Their laughter grew louder, and Timmy felt slowly moving into the background of all that noise and commotion, into his mind, the sounds and sights grew distant as if pushed back by a camera defocus, the inner voices replaced the commotion outside, growing louder, the sneers and jeers were now internal and that was even more humiliating, he wished he could curl up in a a shell like a turtle and disappear but instead his eyes welled up.

He wanted to scream back at them, but instead he found himself crying as he bent down to pick up his belongings.

Drawn by the commotion, Mrs Thompson, the principal, appeared in the corridor. "What's going on here?" she asked Jake in a strict voice.

Jake pointed at Timmy. "Miss, he's making up crazy stories again."

Mrs Thompson looked at Timmy sternly. "Timmy, we've discussed this before. You need to stop fabricating stories. It's a bad habit, and I'm afraid this is turning into one."

Timmy tried to protest with as much strength as he could muster up, "But it's true, Miss! Lythari and I—"

"Enough!" Mrs Thompson interrupted him. "You're disturbing every single student. See me at my office right now." Saying this, she walked away, and Timmy was left in tears as the boys and girls resumed their mocking and jeering.

At the principal's office, Timmy faced a stern lecture. "Your imagination is impressive, I must admit. But of late it has become a problem. You need to focus on reality, else these distractions will hamper your grades. This should be the last time I'm having to talk to you about this."

Timmy nodded helplessly.

But the matter did not end there. Mrs Thompson called Mr and Mrs Tint at her office that afternoon and complained about how their son keeps lying and doesn't let anyone focus at school. She recommended they put him in yoga or see the school counsellor about it. She was very clear , if this continued the school will not entertain.

PRINCIPAL

When Timmy returned home, Mrs Tint asked, "Darling, what happened at school today?"

Timmy recounted the events, holding back his tears. "Believe me Mummy, its true! Lythari and I went on this amazing adventure last night."

Mr Tint sighed. "Listen son, Mummy and I know you are creative, and we deeply appreciate it. But dear, it's high time you learn to separate fantasy from reality. You're not that small a kid anymore, to not know the difference, Timmy."

"We'll talk to Mrs Thompson about finding ways to channelize your creativity in a positive way. Don't worry, darling, we are here for you" Mrs Tint added.

Timmy was frustrated. "You're misunderstanding me. Or maybe, you don't want to understand me in the first place."

His father pulled him into a hug. "We love you son, and we're here to support you. But sometimes, it can be hard to distinguish between dreams and reality. That's all we're saying."

Timmy nodded silently, his heart an ocean of emotions. He knew his adventure was real, but nobody seemed to believe him. He missed Lythari and wished he was here. Lythari would understand.

Timmy trudged to his bedroom, feeling dejected. He flopped onto his bed, staring at the ceiling as the events of the day replayed in his mind. How excitedly he had started his day, and now, as the day was coming to an end, he lay on his bed, lonely and miserable.

Sleep evaded him, and a rollercoaster of emotions took over. He started thinking maybe something *was* wrong with him after all. Maybe everyone was right. Maybe he was, in fact, making up stories....

Around 8 o'clock, Timmy heard two very gentle knocks on his bedroom window. The sound was so soft that had he been asleep he would never have heard it. There was complete silence all around, and his heart skipped a beat as he got down from his bed and went over to the other side of the room.

To be honest, he was scared at first thinking some bird or animal or worse still, a spider may have caused the sound, but the knocks sounded very purposeful and curiosity couldn't allow him to stay back, as curiosity won over fear, Slowly, he drew the curtains and opened the window. Very carefully, very mindfully. He peered outside.

A number of things happened at once. Timmy's heart pounded so fast and loud that Timmy thought he was having a heart attack, then he thought he might be hallucinating. His eyes widened in astonishment, and he slipped on the mat and fell down, hurting his ankle.

Lythari perched on the windowsill, his wings folded, one paw raised in an attempted *Hi*, and eyes twinkling like they were actual stars. With an expression of confusion between Happy and smiling, and, embarrassed at the astonishment he has caused.

Timmy's mind reeled. Now he knew why everyone seemed to think he was lying. Even he couldn't believe what he was seeing.

"Lythari! You're– you're real?" Timmy stammered. His mouth parched dry.

Lythari chuckled. "Of course I am! And honestly, I'm a little offended at your response. I know I live in a realm beyond the mortal world, but that doesn't mean I don't have feelings. I was expecting a heartier welcome, my friend."

Timmy's bewilderment gave way to excitement. He brushed his hands along Lythari's wings. "Oh, come on Lythari! You know what I meant" he laughed, and the Angel laughed along.

Timmy invited his friend onto the terrace, and opening his door as noiselessly as he could, tiptoed up the stairs. Once on the terrace, he saw how unbelievably snowy and sparkly Lythari's fur was. He'd never realised it in his dreams. They sat together, gazing at the star-studded sky.

Lythari's presence seemed surreal and almost unreal. Timmy still couldn't believe he had come all the way from his own world to meet him.

"Thanks for coming, Lythari. I almost started believing you were just a dream" Timmy told him, still grappling with everything that had happened in his life in the last twenty-four hours.

The starry eyes sparkled. "Dreams are but doorways to other realms, dear friend. And our bond transcends the boundaries of an ordinary dream."

Timmy's curiosity overflowed. "But why can't anyone else see you?"

Lythari's expression turned serious. "This world isn't ready for me yet. Humanity's pessimism would harm both our worlds."

Timmy understood. "My parents and everyone at school think I'm crazy."

Lythari nodded. "Exactly. That's because your world values only logic and reason. My existence defies those principles; hence people here think it's a lie."

Timmy looked down. "I feel like I'm living two lives – one in dreams and one in reality."

"You're not alone. Many experience this dichotomy. But not everyone gets to have a friendship like ours. Ours is a unique bond"

Lythari put his paw on Timmy's hand, reassuring him.

Their eyes met. "But why me? Why did you choose me?"

Lythari's wings rustled softly in the breeze. "Because your heart is pure. You see beyond the veil of the rational. I sensed your ability to understand and appreciate my world, something I didn't sense in anybody else. You are a special boy, Timmy. Don't let anybody convince you otherwise."

As they spoke, the night air filled with a sweet, ethereal scent. Timmy felt as if the stars themselves had come down to listen to them.

His thoughts clarified. "I get it. Your secret is safe with me. From now on, it's *our* secret." Lythari smiled. "Thank you, dear friend. Together, we'll navigate both worlds. And when the time is right, perhaps our bond will help bridge the gap between dreams and reality."

Their conversation wove a spell of understanding. Lythari sensed Timmy's internal turmoil. "Tell me, Timmy, what troubles you?"

Timmy looked into the kind eyes of his companion, took a deep breath, and let his emotions flow.

"Today was awful. I tried to tell my friends about last night's adventure, but they laughed at me, mocked me and threw my bag on the floor."

Lythari's floppy ears perked up.

"They said I was making it up, that I was a liar. Even Mrs Thompson didn't believe me. She said I need to focus on reality." His voice cracked. "It hurts, Lythari. They don't understand. They don't see the magic."

Lythari's face softened. "I am here, Timmy. *I* see the magic, and I see *you*."

"And then, she called Mummy and Daddy. Now they too are worried about me. They think I'm losing touch with reality." Timmy's eyes got teary. "But I know I'm not crazy. I know what I see is real. I know you are real."

Lythari beamed. "You are anything but crazy. You are brave, and gifted. You see beyond the veil."

Timmy wiped his eyes. He felt as if a weight had lifted off his heart. "Thanks, Lythari. Both for coming to see me and spending so much time with me. I feel much better now. It's amazing how talking to you feels so easy."

Lythari's wings unfolded slightly, and he drew Timmy in for a hug. "Anytime, young friend! That's what friends are for after all."

While Timmy poured out his heart to his magical confidante, the stars above seemed to twinkle in understanding. The night air seemed to embrace him with empathy. Lythari listened attentively, absorbing every word the little boy spoke. His presence validated Timmy's emotions, and made him feel seen and heard.

Suddenly, Lythari stood up. Unfolding his majestic wings, he declared, "Enough of this sad reality. Tonight, let's soar above the world's doubts and fears."

Timmy's eyes sparkled. There was an immediate shift in the energy. Timmy felt recharged and magically his woes wiped off.

"What! Really? Are you saying what I think you're saying?"

The Angel grinned. He offered his back, and Timmy climbed on, feeling the warmth and softness of his body. With one strong beat, Lythari's wings lifted them far into the night sky. The wind whipped through Timmy's hair as they soared above the city.

THREE

FLIGHT OF FAITH

They glided over gleaming skyscrapers with heads hiding in the clouds like giants. The moon cast a silvery path across the river, leading them to the outskirts of the city. In the distance, a display of fireworks erupted, painting the sky with vibrant colours. Lythari banked and dived, sending Timmy's stomach into delightful flips.

As they flew over a lake, its waters reflected the starry sky like a mirror, creating for Timmy an illusion of flying through the cosmos. Timmy laughed, feeling free and exhilarated. "My God, Lythari! This is incredible!"

Lythari's voice rumbled beneath him. "This world may not understand us, Timmy, but we've got each other."

The sublime creature glided through the night sky. Timmy held tight, his heart racing with excitement. The city unfolded below them like a twinkling tapestry. Streetlights cast a golden glow, and cars moved like tiny, glowing insects.

"This is amazing!" Timmy screamed into the night.

"Brace yourself, young adventurer. We are just getting started!" Lythari's voice echoed.

They swooped over a park, where couples strolled hand-in-hand beneath glimmering string lights. The scent of blooming flowers wafted up, filling Timmy's senses.

Next, Lythari flew over a bustling street. Timmy spotted a group of musicians playing a lively tune on the sidewalk. The music drifted up, harmonizing with the wind. They seemed lost in their art oblivious of the surroundings or worries of daytime, Lythari's wings beat in rhythm, and Timmy could feel the music resonating within him.

Suddenly, another burst of fireworks illuminated the sky, casting a kaleidoscope of colours across the city. Lythari expertly navigated through, and Timmy felt as though he was flying through the very heart of the fireworks. The city's sounds, the car horns, the laughter, the music, all blended into a symphony of joy. Timmy had never experienced anything like this before. Exciting, scary , wonderful, completely novel and full of anticipation all at the same time.

Lythari streamed over a lofty bridge. The Angel's paws pointed to a fleet of ships sailing beneath. Their lights created a shimmering trail on the water.

Timmy gasped. "It's like the magical pathway that we saw on one of our quests!"

Lythari chuckled. "See? Your world is full of magic too. You just need to look for it at the right places."

After an exhilarating flight, that was, for Timmy, a whirlwind of awe and wonder, Lythari gently descended onto a lush meadow beside the riverside.

With a soft pop, he suddenly vanished, leaving Timmy all alone. Timmy's heart skipped a beat. He frantically looked around, whispering, "Lythari? Lythari, where are you?"

A reassuring whisper echoed inside his mind. "I am *here*, Timmy. With you. Don't worry."

Timmy relaxed, sensing his companion's presence. He strolled through the meadow, and the scent of fresh grass and wildflowers filled the air.

The riverside meadow unfolded like a serene oasis beside the gently flowing river. Soft grass, emerald green and inviting, stretched towards the water's edge, where willows and cottonwoods stood sentinel. Wildflowers swayed in the breeze, their vibrant hues – lavender, yellow, and pink – danced amidst the lush foliage. The air vibrated with the sweet songs of crickets and the occasional hoot of an owl. A wooden dock jutted into the river, weathered to a silvery grey hue. Fish swam lazily beneath the surface, their scales shining like diamonds in the moonlight. Timmy noticed that beneath the starry sky, the meadow seemed transformed into an enchanted haven. Fireflies glowed like tiny lanterns, lighting the way for the creatures of night. The river's gentle lapping against the shore created a soothing melody, harmonizing with the rustling leaves and chirping insects.

In one corner, a yellow snack-van stood parked. The aroma of sizzling corndogs and crispy fries wafted through the air, enticing passers-by.

As Timmy strolled through the meadow, he felt the soft earth beneath his feet, as if trying to whisper to him the night's secrets. He approached the snack-van, where late-night workers were hustling.

"Corndogs, Lythari?" Timmy whispered softly to his invisible friend. "Yes, please! I'm starving" the wind seemed to whisper back.

The corndogs! Golden-brown and crispy on the outside, juicy and tasty on the inside, they were the epitome of culinary delight. Juicy skewered hot dogs, made from premium beef and pork, were carefully wrapped in a delicate layer of cornmeal batter, fried to perfection. Their sizzling aroma wafted through the air, teasing Timmy's senses and tantalizing his taste buds.

"Two Classic Corndog Delights please!" Timmy said confidently, addressing the workers who were just about to close for the day.

The men looked up at him, taken aback at a little boy ordering two whole corndogs late in the evening all by himself.

Sensing their confusion, Timmy said immediately, "Oh I'll take it home for me and my sister to eat." adding a convincing smile when deep inside he felt awkward at the lie, scared of being caught and reported to his parents.

At this, the men seemed to relax a bit, although they still looked pretty unconvinced. They turned around and became busy preparing Timmy's order.

Suddenly, Timmy felt a tap on his shoulder. Looking back, he saw no one, but he felt as if he heard a faint whisper in his ears that said, "Well done, Timmy! I'm so proud of you. I knew you could do this by yourself. Now if you will look inside your pockets," the whisper ceased. Timmy put his hands inside his pockets, and at once felt some money.

"Oh my God," he said to himself, "I'd almost forgotten about the payment part." He felt a soft laughter near his ears, and smiled.

After having received his order and paid for the same, Timmy made sure to walk a considerable distance from the crowded street into a quiet corner, where Lythari and he indulged in the delicious corndogs topped with a dollop of creamy mustard, a sprinkle of paprika, and a dash of chopped onions. Each bite yielded a satisfying crunch, giving way to the savour within, and leaving them craving for more. Once they were done, Timmy started walking along the riverside, enjoying the peaceful night, and talking to Lythari in his mind, about how crazy the entire experience had been for him so far.

Suddenly, Timmy heard someone call from behind, "Hey boy! Why are you walking alone so late in the evening?" He turned around, and saw two police officers rushing towards him, a concerned look on their faces. "What do you think you're doing out here, huh?" one of them shouted.

Timmy's eyes widened in fear. "I– I was just– "

Even before he could think of another convincing lie to feed the officers, Timmy felt his body lifted up in the wind in one powerful swoop, as if by some invisible force. Lythari. "Uh-oh," Timmy said, nervously glancing at the people on the street.

As the officers came running towards Timmy, their expressions changed from concern to astonishment, and then horror.

"What the– " one of them trailed off, eyes wide as a goblet.

"Did he just– " the other started, pointing at the sky with one hand and scratching his head with another.

Their faces contorted with confusion, as they watched Timmy fly away on an invisible Lythari's back.

People crowded all around, heads peeked from balconies. Hearing the chaos that had suddenly erupted, four more officers came running down the street, and looking up at the sky, were overcome with a feeling that was somewhere between astonishment and terror.

"What in the name of Christ is happening?" one of them asked, confusion etched on his face.

Another officer fumbled for his radio, attempting to call for more backup. "We need to, uh, report a, a *flying child*." he stuttered.

For a moment, they all stood frozen, unsure how to react, as Timmy and Lythari vanished into the night sky. Finally, one officer shook his head and snapped out of the trance. "Get the cameras, idiots! We need evidence!" But by the time mobiles and cameras emerged and they managed to aim the lenses, the *flying child* was a mere speck on the horizon.

They all exchanged horrified, bewildered looks, and soon, whispers of "flying boy" and "incredible sighting" erupted in the street and spread through the police radio.

As Timmy soared through the night sky on Lythari's back, his palpitating heart slowly calmed, breathing normalised and his emotion switched from fear to that of exhilaration.

Relief washed over him, knowing he had evaded the police; he could never have made the officers believe him.

"Woo-hoo!" he cried, grinning from ear to ear. "Yay! But hold tight, Timmy" Lythari's invisible form chuckled beneath him.

The wind rushed past, whipping Timmy's hair into a frenzy. He felt free, free from the constraints of the world below. His heart pounded with excitement. "We did it, Lythari! We outran them! Or should I say, out-*flew*, ha-ha!" Timmy exclaimed. Lythari's wings beat stronger, responding to Timmy's enthusiasm.

Together, they pierced the clouds, leaving the rational world and its concerns far behind.

When Timmy saw his house approaching in the distance, nothing but gratitude filled his innocent heart. The excitement of adventure and exploration felt good, but returning to the safety of his home felt even better. "Thanks, Lythari. I owe you one."

Lythari's gentle voice whispered to him in the wind, "Anytime, Timmy. Your safety is my priority."

Timmy spotted his bedroom window, and a sense of peace settled over him. The night's adventures replayed in his mind. The flight, the corndogs, the narrow escape.

A smile spread across his face. Looking down at his feet wrapped around an invisible blanket of air, he took a deep breath. "Best. Night ever " Timmy exhaled into the night air.

"So Far" Lythari corrected him.

Gently, Lythari deposited his friend on the sill of his bedroom window. "Sweet dreams, Timmy" the Angel whispered. Then, raising his paw in another adorable gesture of a goodbye, he took off.

Timmy watched him fly as he disappeared into the horizon. With a happy heart and a mind still soaring with the thrill of the night, he drifted off into deep, peaceful slumber.

● 25 ●

FOUR
MISSED DEADLINES AND EMBARRASSMENT

The next morning, the Tint household buzzed with excitement.

"Have you seen this? 'Mysterious Flying Boy' is all over the news!" Mrs Tint was scanning her phone, as she sipped her coffee.

Looking up from the newspaper, her husband grunted. "Probably some prank or mass hysteria."

Mrs Tint continued, "The police are baffled. They claim they saw a young boy fly away from them last night as they were about to ask him what he was doing on the streets all alone."

Timmy's eyes sparkled with excitement, and a hint of a smile played on his lips, though he tried to keep his face composed. But when his father dismissed the story, the grin subsided, and was soon replaced by an indifferent, almost amused expression. His mother asked him what he thought about the news, and Timmy's eyes darted briefly to his father, then back to his mother. He shrugged.

Internally, however, Timmy was feeling a lot of emotions. He was relieved that his secret was safe, amused at his father's scepticism, somewhere grateful for his mother's curiosity that was evidence of her open-mindedness, and excited as he remembered Lythari and all the things they had done the previous night.

The Tints enjoyed a hearty breakfast. Scrambled eggs with crispy bacon, golden-brown pancakes with strawberries and whipped cream, and freshly squeezed orange juice. Timmy savoured each bite, his mind going back and forth between the news and his nocturnal escapade with Lythari. Mrs Tint appeared absent-minded, while Mr Tint crunched on bacon, his face a mask of nonchalance.

Suddenly, he scoffed. "Tired cops mistook a kid on a skateboard for a flying boy. Media sensationalism."

Mrs Tint chuckled. "You're not impressed, dear?"

"Until I see concrete evidence, I won't believe this nonsense, nothing interesting has happened in this town anytime recently, the media has to have something for the people to talk about" came a stern response.

Timmy, knowing the truth, smiled. Once he finished his breakfast, Mrs Tint turned to him.

"Timmy, what do you think? Could it be possible?"

Timmy shrugged again. Trying his best to keep the excitement in his voice down. "Dunno, Mummy. But it sure sounds crazy."

Mr Tint nodded in approval.

Suddenly, Timmy felt as if his mother winked at him. She said, "Maybe you'll solve the mystery, Timmy."

Timmy's heart skipped a beat, but he was sure it was a mistake. His secret was definitely safe.

While getting ready for school, his mind replayed the thrill of the previous night. As he showered, he imagined Lythari's magnificent wings soaring through the sky and recalled the wind rushing past his ears. He chuckled as the horrified looks on the officers' faces crossed his mind.

He put on his favourite superhero T-shirt, feeling like a real-life hero, and envisioned himself saving Lythari someday in the same way the Angel had swooped in to rescue him last night. He grabbed his backpack, and stuffed in his books and folders, his mind entirely on the riverside meadow, where he and Lythari had shared corndogs.

He headed downstairs. "Don't forget your lunch, Timmy!" Mrs Tint called from the kitchen.

He grabbed the lunchbox unmindfully, kept on the table, and was reminded of the snack van and the puzzled looks on the faces of the men as Timmy tricked them. He laughed. Then kissing his mother goodbye, he headed out the door.

As soon as he stepped onto the school bus, the chatter was palpable:

"Did you hear about the flying boy?"

"I know, right? It's like a superhero movie!"

"How does that even work? It's unbelievable. It's a pity they didn't get pictures."

Emma spotted Timmy quietly taking his seat and hurried over. "Hey! What's up?" she asked, eyes almost bulging out with curiosity.

"Just the usual" Timmy replied.

Emma leaned in, her voice barely above a whisper but full of humour, in a sing song tone she chimed . "I know it's you, Timmy. The flying boy, I'm sure about it."

"Don't be ridiculous, Emma," Timmy said with a chuckle. "I'm not exactly *flying material*."

Emma raised an eyebrow, sounding funny and convincing at the same time in an attempt to pull out the truth. "You're always disappearing at night, and now this happens. You think I can't connect the dots?", she giggled.

Timmy's face remained impassive. "Well, I mean, it could just be a coincidence. Besides, I was home all night yesterday."

"Well, I wish, I'm the simplest of all simpletons, and happy at that but having a famous best friend wouldn't hurt" she chuckled mischievously and innocently in a cheerful voice .

Timmy pursed his lips in a gesture that the topic is to be dropped and sharply looked out of the window with a swift jerk of his neck.

Emma's eyes narrowed, she made a gesture of 'I'm watching you' ,but she dropped the subject and went back to her seat to re-join the on-going conversation. Timmy looked outside the window, his ears buzzing with what everybody had to say about his adventure.

"I heard the police saw him flying over the river" one of the boys said.

"My dad says it's fake news. Just another sham to increase their viewership, you know" said another.

"I wish I could fly!" said one of the girls, gesturing flying with her hands spread across and zooming between the seats of the moving bus to fall flat on her face. All of them broke into giggles collectively.

Timmy smiled. It felt good to be the only one knowing the truth. Periodically, he could sense Emma's stupidly curious and suspicious glance on him, but he kept up the charade, protecting Lythari and their secret.

The excitement was still in the air when the bus arrived at school. All this while, Timmy's mind had been preoccupied with Lythari and their time together, but now he saw Emma walking over to him with a smirk and eyebrows raised. "Now what is she guessing" – Timmy's mind spoke to himself.

"Did you finish the Social Science project, Timmy?" she asked swaying her head animatedly and puckering her lips.

Emma's question hit him like a rock. His heart sank, and he felt his stomach twisting into knots. He knew he had done the project, but he couldn't recall putting it in his school bag that morning.

He frantically scanned his backpack, rummaging through the books and folders. *Oh no, oh no, oh no!* He had left the file at home in his morning haze and rush.

Panic set in as he realized what was to come. The entire class would be laughing at him, and he would receive a good thrashing from Mrs Johnson. His face flushed, and droplets of sweat appeared on his forehead.

"Uh I– uh– I think I– forgot, Emma" Timmy stammered.

Emma's eyes widened, mischief now replaced with true concern. "Timmy, how could you forget? It's due today! What were you doing last night?"

Timmy shrugged, trying to hide his embarrassment and frustration.

"I know, I know. I have it ready. I had put so much effort into it. I was just– um– well I was a bit distracted yesterday" he muttered.

Emma sighed, but didn't push the matter, the perfect mix of innocence and maturity, she knew it would only further his embarrassment. "Okay okay. Let's go to class now. You can ask Mrs Johnson for an extension and see what she says."

Timmy nodded, a little relieved that Emma didn't push the subject of last night. But he was still reeling from his mistake, and as they walked to class, Timmy felt extremely disappointed in himself.

Why had he been so careless? Why had he not double-checked his bag? Lythari's appearance had consumed his thoughts to such an extent that it had made him forget important responsibilities and deadlines. As he prepared himself for another horrible day at school, he made a silent promise to himself. He vowed to stay focused and avoid such mistakes in the future, no matter how thrilling and fun his life got.

FIVE

EMMA'S SUSPICION GROWS

Mrs Johnson's was the very first class. Once she was done reviewing the agenda for the day, her sharp eyes scanned the room. "Alright, students, please pass forward your social science projects that were due today."

Timmy's anxiety grew. He had never wished more to become invisible.

Emma nudged him. "Go ask her, silly. She might just extend the deadline for you, you're one of the smartest students in the class, after all. She'll definitely consider"

Timmy took a deep breath and approached Mrs Johnson's desk as slowly as he could. Each step seemed to be heavier than the one before, his breathing became more forced as he tried to keep it normal, his palms turned sweaty and throat dried up as he licked his lips repeatedly in anticipation of the conversation that was about to follow...

The teacher looked at him with a puzzled expression. "What happened, Timmy? Is everything alright,, are you feeling unwell?" she asked in a kind tone.

Hearing the kindness in her voice, Timmy was so embarrassed that he could hardly speak. "Um, Mrs Johnson, I, uh, actually, left my project at home" he admitted apologetically.

Mrs Johnson's expression turned stern. "How could you forget? It was due today. I've been reminding you guys about it since last Monday. Even yesterday I came to the class and gave you all a reminder. Didn't I, students?" The entire class nodded.

Timmy wished he could just disappear into thin air. "I'm really sorry, Miss. I got distracted, and I forgot to pack it. But I have done it, really."

The teacher sighed, her tone changed, she lowered her voice as she addressed only him. "Timmy, you're never like this. You're always so responsible. What happened this time?"

Timmy hesitated, not sure how much to reveal.

"I just had a– an *interesting* night, and the deadline just slipped my mind."

Mrs Johnson raised her eyebrows. "An interesting night?" she said, drawing double quotes in the air with her fingers.

"Just family stuff, Miss" Timmy added a little too hurriedly, embarrassment etched on his face.

Mrs Johnson studied him for a moment before responding loudly again. "Alright, Timmy. I'll give you an extension until tomorrow. But please get your priorities straight. And if you fail to turn it in tomorrow, I'm afraid I'll have to give your project an F."

Timmy exhaled in relief. "Thank you, Mrs Johnson. I promise this won't happen again."

"Yeah, it better not" Mrs Johnson said sternly.

Timmy speeded back to his seat.

No sooner had he returned to his seat than Emma leaned in and whispered to him, "What happened last night?"

Timmy didn't know what to say, and was thankful when Mrs Johnson, having received the projects, tapped on her desk and guided the class back to the lessons.

During the lunch break, a determined Emma cornered Timmy. He was sitting in the school cafeteria, surrounded by the hum of chatter and clinking utensils, when she came running and took the seat right next to him. Their lunch consisted of turkey and cheese sandwich, carrot sticks with hummus, and two glasses of iced tea.

For a while, she didn't say anything, and Timmy decided not to raise the topic by himself.

As he began eating, he observed the other students around, who were engaged in various activities. Some played card games while others sat with their heads together, probably working on their group projects.

Four girls sat at the table beside Timmy's, sharing stories about their weekends and bursting into laughter occasionally.

A group of senior boys discussed strategies for their upcoming football match. Not very far from them, there was a cluster of students huddled around a boy who appeared to be reading something out from the day's newspaper that sent the others in frequent *Ooh*'s and *Woah*'s. No points for guessing what they're reading, Timmy thought.

He saw the cafeteria staff busy replenishing food stations and cleaning the tables, and turned his focus back to the food.

He could still constantly feel Emma's side glances at him…

" What? Do I have a a ketchup moustache? Why are you staring?" He knew what she was thinking, but a desperate attempt to divert.

"Timmy, I know it's you, the flying boy" Emma said all of a sudden, and Timmy was so startled he almost choked on his food.

"You're crazy" he said, chewing his food. Not meeting her eye.

Emma leaned in, her face inches from Timmy's. "I saw the news that's gone viral on the news. The flying boy's build, hair colour, it's definitely you." She said gravely, not blinking.

Timmy's mind raced; he needed a convincing lie. He knew this girl since they were inseparable toddlers, he knew even if he could convince Mummy Daddy or Grandma, there was no escape from her razor sharp tiny brain.

"Okay, fine. I'll tell you what I know. But it's not me," Timmy said faking a serious expression. "I know someone who knows the flying boy."

Emma's eyes widened. "Well, who?" she added an accent and made a face.

Timmy took a deep breath as he spun the tale in his head. "My cousin Alex. He is friends with him. They met at a summer camp."

Emma's curiosity piqued. Her voice high pitched now, making small seated jumps and hands clutched together, with an expression mocking an animated movie character "What's his name?", she made the words, her chords and eyebrows dance in sync.

"Alex. I just told you" Timmy said, trying to avoid the question.

"No silly. The flying boy's, I meant" Emma replied determinedly. She was in the story, invested completely. Timmy was winning.

Timmy raced his thoughts. "Dave! Dave Wells."

Emma nodded, but she didn't look convinced. "What's Dave's story?" she brushed off as if investigating a crime.

At this, Timmy realised that unless he gives Emma a convincing answer to her question, there was no escape for him. He improvised on his story, weaving an imaginative narrative.

"You see, Dave's family is originally from Europe. They moved here last year. His parents are scientists, and they discovered a...a flying serum."

Emma's eyes sparkled. "A flying serum?" she whispered in a husked up voice, rolling on the 'm'.

Timmy nodded. "Yeah. They've been flying around for years. Dave's family was hiding it all this while, which is why I didn't want to tell you any of it. It's a pity that it's all over the news now. But hey, at least they don't know who the boy is. That's a relief" he gave out a soft laugh.

Emma's face lit up. "Oh my God, Timmy. That's amazing! And I promise to not let your, well, Dave's, secret out."

Timmy smiled, proud of his work. "Thanks Emma, for understanding."

"No problem. But I want to meet Dave! Can you arrange that? Please?" her eyes sparked, her enthusiasm grew. Her seated jumps now creating small earthquakes across the table drawing attention.

Now this was something Timmy hadn't thought of. His lie was about to backfire. "Um, well, I don't know if that's possible" he hedged.

Emma's face fell. She persisted, "Come on, please. I promise I'll keep his secret." She pleaded dramatically.

Timmy scrambled for an excuse. "No just that, Dave is, really private. And his parents are overprotective due to the secrecy of the whole situation. More so now than ever, because of the sighting and all."

Emma nodded understandingly, fully immersed in the story. "Oh yes. I get it. But can't you just ask him once? I promise to not– "

"Emma," Timmy cut her off. "They are moving away actually. His family received threats from their neighbours, who are the only people that know about the serum, wanting to use it for themselves."

Emma looked concerned. "That's terrible!"

Timmy seized the opportunity. "I know. Dave's family is going into witness protection. I won't be able to contact him anytime soon."

At this, Emma was crestfallen. Timmy feigned sympathy. He did love his best friend but knew she was this weird mix of innocence and empathy that was reserved just for him. He didn't want her to feel bad. "Hey, don't be sad. I mean, I'm sad too. But we have to respect their decision."

Emma nodded reluctantly. She ate her food in silence, and once done, gave Timmy a slight nod and walked away. Timmy let out a deep sigh of relief. For now, he had dodged the bullet. He didn't feel too good about lying to Emma, particularly because she was one of the few people at school who talked to him, but he knew it was inevitable. "If that's what it takes to protect Lythari's secret and keep my promise to him, I shall do it again." he said to himself.

SIX

KARATE, LESSONS OF DISCIPLINE AND A REGULAR DAY

After school that day, Timmy headed to the dojo for his karate practice, in much need of some unwinding.

While he was changing into his uniform, he heard the buzz about the flying boy fill the air:

"Dude that kid was actually flying. I watched the video multiple times!" one boy was saying.

"Did you? I couldn't make out much from that tape, but it definitely looked suspicious" another agreed.

Timmy tried to feign disinterest, but inside, his stomach was making flips, and not in the good way. He simultaneously felt a surge of excitement and a hint of anxiety, worried someone might connect the dots.

At that moment, Sensei Sam , their instructor, cleared his throat, and announced the beginning of the day's lessons. "Alright, students! Warm-up time! Let's get those kicks and punches ready."

As they stretched and jogged, the "flying boy" conversation continued:

"You think that kid is here amongst us?"

"In karate? Nah, he's probably too busy saving the world." All of them started laughing.

Sensei Sam heard them. "Focus, students! Karate isn't about flying or superpowers. It's discipline, respect, and self-control. So, make sure your mind is not somewhere else" he intervened, in a military voice and tone, giving a quick side-glance at the boy who had raised the topic.

They fell silent, and everyone focused on their practice. The dojo's warm glow enveloped Timmy as he took his position for the warm-up jog. The sensei clapped twice, and the class sprang into action. Timmy felt his feet pounding the floor in unison with his peers, and as they transitioned from jogging to jumping jacks, sweat began to trickle down his face.

This was followed by dynamic stretching- leg swings, arm circles, and torso twists. Timmy's muscles loosened, preparing him for the intense practice ahead.

"Kihon time!" Sensei Sam announced.

The students lined up, facing the mirrors. Timmy assumed the first stance, feet shoulder-width apart. Sensei walked along the line, correcting postures and offering words of encouragement to the students. "Punch!" he said to Timmy. Timmy's fist shot out, his arm extending in a perfect straight line. "*Ki-ah!*" he exclaimed, releasing a burst of energy.

The class continued, mastering various kicks, blocks, and strikes. Timmy's focus wavered briefly, the image of Lythari's wings fluttering in his mind. Sensei noticed. "Timmy, keep your mind present! Concentrate on your technique."

Timmy nodded his head, in an attempt to clear. Refocused, executing each move with precision.

After Kihon, the class moved on to Kata. Timmy's feet glided across the mat, his arms weaving an intricate tapestry of blocks and strikes.

Sparring came next. Timmy faced his partner, bowing respectfully. The match began, each opponent exchanging blows and counterattacks. His heart raced, adrenaline coursing through his veins.

The final segment, cool-down, brought tranquillity. Static stretches relaxed Timmy's muscles, his mind calming as he meditated.

Sensei Sam approached him, a warm smile on his face. "Good job today, Timmy" he said, patting Timmy's shoulder. Timmy beamed with pride.

This is some redemption from my irresponsible behaviour day at school today, he thought.

Timmy walked into the house, greeted by the savoury aroma of dinner.

After washing up and changing into his pyjamas he headed downstairs imagining himself to be magically carried down by the waft of freshly cooked food...

Mr Tint was setting the table. "Hey, honey! How was your day?" he asked in a cheerful voice.

Timmy took a deep breath. "Mummy, Daddy, I need to apologize for something."

Mr Tint's expression turned serious. He exchanged a curious glance with his wife, who was sitting at the dinner table and pouring water into the glasses.

"What is it, sweetie?" Mrs Tint asked.

"I forgot my social science project at home today. And today was the deadline," Timmy admitted, his eyes downcast. But when he heard no response from his parents, he looked up, and quickly added sheepishly, to cover up, "But she agreed to extend the deadline till tomorrow." He forced a smile masking his embarrassment.

Mrs Tint, who had been figuring out a stern yet kind way to respond to her son's apology, now heaved a sigh of relief. "That's okay, dear. We all forget sometimes." Mr Tint nodded and resumed serving the food.

Timmy continued, "And Emma thought *I* was the flying boy! Can you believe it?"

This time, both his parents stopped what they were doing midway, and looked at each other one more time. "What?" Timmy asked.

Mr Tint chuckled. "Well, you do have a knack for adventure, son." His eyes crinkling up at the joke.

Timmy smiled sheepishly. "Well yeah, but it's not me, right? And she wouldn't believe me. So I had to come up with a pretty wild story to convince her otherwise."

His mom raised one eyebrow at him. "Do tell. We love your imaginative telling, you remember, when you were smaller grandma recorded one of your made up stories about that hungry man lost in woods who ate insects to survive? I'll call her after dinner which reminds me"

Timmy flushed, embarrassed, " ya mom, I remember that, actually grandma had told me something similar, I built up on that, don't remind me, that was so stupid" he then recounted his made-up tale about Dave and the flying serum. His parents listened attentively, amused. When he was finished, all Mr Tint said was "Flying serum and all. I think you did a pretty good at job *convincing* her, Timmy" emphasizing the word "convincing." Then he glanced at his wife, who was trying hard to maintain a straight face. The rest of the dinner was eaten in complete silence.

Once they were done eating, Timmy thought of breaking the awkward silence by telling his parents about his karate lesson.

"Sensei reminded us that karate is about discipline and self-control, not just physical moves" he said, looking at his father.

Mr Tint nodded. "That's great. You're learning valuable life skills."

"How was sparring today?" Mrs Tint joined in.

"Intense. But I kept my focus and executed some awesome kicks. Sensei Sam said I did a good job today" Timmy replied excitedly.

His parents smiled. "We're proud of you, Timmy," Mrs Tint said. "Not just for karate, but for owning up to your mistakes."

Timmy smiled back at them, feeling grateful for his loving family.

The evening drew to a close, and Timmy began his bedtime routine. He trudged upstairs, his legs feeling heavy from the day's activities. Before brushing his teeth, he glanced at his backpack, sprawled on the floor from when he had come to his room to change.

A sudden surge of responsibility washed over him. He hastily grabbed the social science project from his desk, and after scanning through the pages, tucked it into his backpack. "Can't forget that again!" he muttered to himself.

Next, he double-checked his schedule for the next day. Karate practice was cancelled, but he had math homework due tomorrow. He opened the notebook, and to his relief, saw that he had already done it. He packed it along with his math and English textbooks, ensuring everything was in order.

Having organized his backpack, Timmy felt a sense of accomplishment. He changed into comfortable sleep pyjamas and brushed his teeth, his eyes growing heavy. As he climbed into bed, his thoughts drifted to Lythari and their aerial adventure.

A contented smile spread across his face. The excitement of the day, combined with physical exhaustion, soon took its toll. Timmy's eyelids drooped, and he snuggled deeper into his blankets.

The last thing he remembered was the soothing hum of his alarm clock signalling his bedtime. Then, the house grew quiet, and the only sound was the distant hum of crickets outside. Darkness enveloped him, and he drifted off to sleep.

SEVEN

MERLAND

Timmy found himself standing on a sunlit beach, crisp warm sand between his toes.

Lythari, majestic and radiant as always, stood beside him. Together, they gazed out at the turquoise ocean, waves gently lapping at the shore.

"Tonight, we venture into the tropical undersea" Lythari announced, spreading his wings wide for Timmy to climb up.

With one loud scream of excitement, Timmy grasped Lythari's soft, warm body. Sometimes he wished to ask Lythari to fly for a longer while than usual, just so he can sit on his cosy back for some more time. But that would be too selfish, he thought, and he didn't want to cause his dear friend any unnecessary pain.

Lythari lifted his paws off the ground, with a comfortable Timmy hugging him tight. They soared above the waves, descending into the crystal-clear waters. Schools of fish of various colours darted past them in the pattern of a very impromptu dance. Coral reefs teemed with life, and vibrant sea anemones waved in the current.

Magically Timmy's diving gear appeared.

As Timmy and Lythari entered the ocean realm, they encountered a playful blue dolphin named Finley, who swam alongside them, clicking his beak and whistling. Timmy was just about to ask Lythari what he was trying to say, when the Angel translated, "Finley welcomes us to the underwater realm."

Timmy grinned. "Thanks, Finley. I had only seen dolphins in pictures before, so that makes you my first dolphin friend!"

Finley chirped, and Timmy knew the dolphin was smiling at him. He clicked his beak again, and Lythari said, "Finley wants us to follow him. He says he's very pleased to meet you and cannot wait for you to explore his beautiful home."

Timmy smiled. "I'm ready, Lythari. Let's go!"

Finley guided them through a coral maze, where he introduced them to Crusty, a wise sea-turtle, who shared with them tales of the ocean's depths having confused many an experienced explorer.

But Timmy had no fears. "Don't worry, Crusty. I've got Lythari with me," he said, and looked down at his friend, who smiled back at him and nodded. With a hearty "Thank you, Finley and Crusty!" they departed for the magical kingdom of Merland.

As Crusty had mentioned to them, there was a huge purple gate and magnificent purple walls surrounding the kingdom. An invisible orb of sparkly shimmery sea water encased the entirety of Merland that casted a pearly glow to the surroundings.

Once they approached the gate, Lythari touched his wings to it, and whispered in a language unknown to Timmy, and it flew open gently revealing the beauty of what lay inside.

As soon as they entered, Timmy was mesmerized at the view. The water here was lighter than air and clearer than crystal, Merland glowed with colours nobody had seen before – turquoise rocks, lilac seashells, and silver sparkling sand. The coral reefs stretched for miles, arching up like castles with towers of pink, blue, and orange. Shimmering schools of fish, glowing jellyfish, and friendly seahorses swirled around cheerfully.

Timmy and Lythari ventured deeper, Timmy's eyes simultaneously dazzled by all the colours and wide with awe and astonishment. Suddenly, he saw something in the distance that made his heart skip. "Look, Lythari! Mermaids!"

Lythari laughed. "Ha-ha! They are the Merfolk, Timmy, and tonight we shall explore their kingdom. But make sure you're respectful. The Merfolk hate disrespect." Timmy nodded understandingly. "Of course, Lythari, of course."

As Lythari approached them, Timmy saw that the Merfolk looked exactly like the mythical mermaids in his art book. They had long, flowing tails in every colour of the rainbow, and they were wearing crowns made from seashells and necklaces of pearls.

Seeing Timmy and Lythari, one of them came forward and greeted them.

"Welcome, travellers! I am Luna. Queen Calypso awaits you."

Timmy, who had no idea who Queen Calypso was, looked at Lythari, confused.

Lythari's face was lit up. "This must be a really special one for him," he said to himself.

They arrived at the Mer Palace, a dazzling wonder nestled at the heart of Merland's reefs and built from the largest and most lustrous pearls in the ocean. The Palace shimmered with an ethereal glow, casting soft rainbows that danced across the surrounding water. Towers spiralled high like seashells reaching towards the surface, and delicate pearl bridges connected each tower, twisting gracefully over coral gardens below. The walls were lined with sparkling mother-of-pearl, capturing the light of bioluminescent sea plants that glowed softly in blues, pinks, and greens.

As Timmy and Lythari entered the Throne Hall, Timmy saw a giant coral throne covered in glistening pearls and starry sapphires sitting atop a raised dais.

Queen Calypso was waiting for them on the throne, and she welcomed them warmly.

"Lythari, it's an honour to finally meet you. I've heard so much about you and your adventures. And Timmy, your curiosity is renowned in the entire kingdom."

Timmy blushed. "Thank you, Your Majesty."

Queen Calypso smiled. Then she began, "Coralina's history spans across millennia. Our ancestors built this kingdom using ancient magic and harmony with the sea."

"How do you maintain secrecy from the surface world?" Lythari asked.

The Queen's smile faltered just a little, as she regained her graceful smile.

"We have developed powerful spells to conceal our presence. Otherwise, humans, with their dirty intentions and cruel actions, will not let us live in peace. They have a history of harming the innocent. Only those humans with pure hearts and genuine intentions can find us" she said, and her kind eyes rested on Timmy. "Like you, Timmy."

Timmy's eyes widened. "I am honoured, Your Majesty" he replied. He realised the gleamy glistening orb around the city must be the spells She was mentioning about.

Right then, one of the younger Merfolk spoke up, "We also have the Guardians of the Reef, brave Merfolk warriors who protect our borders in case any human dares to come to the kingdom. But that does not happen very often. No matter how brave they claim to be, innately humans are all cowards. They fear for their lives more than anything else."

Timmy nodded. "Yes that's true, we understand" he admitted shamefully.

"Your kingdom's safety is of paramount importance" Lythari agreed. "Some secrets are best kept as secrets, everyone knowing everything only ruins the magic"

Queen Calypso nodded in agreement and continued, "I hope you do not mind the angry undertone in Aria's voice, Timmy," referring to the young mermaid who had just spoken. "But we cannot help it. We have observed humanity's relationship with the ocean. Oil spills, digging of the ocean floor, exploitation of the ocean resources, killing baby fish before even they learn to swim properly, using the ocean as a Dump yard, plastics everywhere. We hope they will learn to respect and preserve our world."

"We read these in our environmental studies class, but how can I change that?" Timmy asked thoughtfully.

Aria smiled. "Share your experiences. Inspire others to cherish the ocean, not destroy and disrespect it. When you speak up, others shall follow."

Timmy nodded again. The words of Lythari during one of their quests echoed in his mind:

Heroism also means having the courage to move forward despite life's obstacles.

What matters is the reflection of your soul. Look within yourself, and you'll know the truth.

As the night wore on, Timmy and Lythari learned more about Merland's magical energy sources, innovative agriculture and their artistic traditions. The Merfolk's laughter and warmth enveloped them, and they heard lots of interesting stories from the older Mermen. Timmy had never paid as much attention in any of his classes as he did to those tales of shipwrecks and pirates and lost seamen. He felt like he could listen to the Merfolk's lore for hours. But after a while, Aria proposed to him and Lythari to take a look at the other parts of the kingdom, and they agreed.

Aria guided them through the winding streets. "Observe our architecture," she said, "It's all corals and shells."

Timmy grinned. He felt overwhelmed with the kingdom's beauty.

On their way, they passed by some Merfolk farmers tending to lush seaweed gardens, Merfolk artisans crafting intricate shell jewellery, and Merfolk children playing with the rainbow fish, who, Timmy supposed, were their friends. Oh, how he wished to be one of them!

Aria led them to one of the craft shops, named *Tides and Treasures*.

It was owned by Delphi, a beautiful mermaid. Upon seeing them, Delphi waved her pink tail and welcomed them inside. "Ah, Lythari and Timmy. I've heard so much about you two" she said, her voice was so musical that Timmy thought she would break into a song at any moment. Timmy was surprised at how many Merfolk knew the two of them!

"Delphi's artistry is known and praised all across the ocean" Aria informed them, appreciative.

Delphi smiled. "I create from the heart, using the ocean's treasures. That's the reason. Wait, let me show you some of my creations."

She pointed to the hundreds of shelves attached to the walls of the shop, waved her tail at the, and some of the shelves opened, their contents floating swiftly outside. She caught them in her hands, and laid them out on the table for Timmy and Lythari to see.

There were intricately carved mother-of-pearl boxes, sea-glass sculptures reflecting the ocean's hues, woven seaweed baskets, coral quills and parchments made from the leaves of the bioluminescent plants that Timmy had spotted at the Mer Palace.

He marvelled. "Your work is stunning!"

Delphi's kind eyes sparkled with gratitude. "Every piece tells a story, inspired by Merland's history and rich tradition" she said, smiling at Timmy.

Timmy wished he could stay longer to listen to those stories but time bound them. His eyes big with wonder, all he could manage to mutter was a faint 'wow'.

They left the craft shop to visit the Merland Refinery next, where Lythari's curiosity was piqued.

"This is where the Merfolk transform human waste into pearls" Aria explained.

The refinery's manager, Orion, greeted them. "We collect garbage from the human world," he said to Lythari and Timmy, "and recycle it into valuable resources."

Timmy watched in awe plastic bottles being broken down into micro-particles which were infused into oyster shells. "The oysters, nurtured by the Merfolk, produce magical luminous pearls," Orion explained, "and these pearls not only beautify our kingdom but also support life here in the depths by providing us habitats." "Moreover," he continued, "they help filter pollutants from the water and enhance ocean currents and circulation. By transforming waste into treasure, we reduce ocean pollution, promote sustainability, and preserve our ecosystem, and we live in the hope that humans learn to do the same someday."

Lythari raised his wings in agreement. "Your ingenuity benefits both worlds. But it's not just your duty. We should all be in this together."

"This process helps the ocean and teaches humans a valuable lesson. I'll keep that lesson in mind, Orion" Timmy promised.

Once they had concluded their tour, Aria took them back to the Palace to meet the Queen for one last time before they left. On entering, they found Queen Calypso standing at the centre of the Throne Hall, watering the plants herself. Seeing them, she stepped forward and smiled.

"The secrets of Merland are now yours too. I humbly request you to not share these with anyone outside the realms of the ocean. That would create a lot of problems for us here. I hope you understand" she said gently.

Both Timmy and Lythari nodded. "Yes, Your Majesty, we understand."

As they prepared to leave, the Queen asked Timmy to put his hand forward, and when he did, she placed a shell-pendant on his palm.

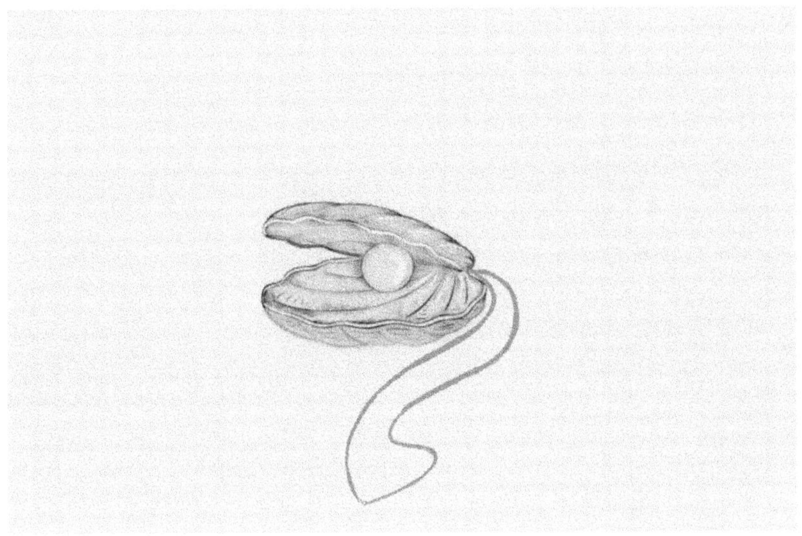

"A symbol of our friendship and shared secrets" she smiled at him.

Timmy smiled back. "I'll treasure this and keep your kingdom's secrets safe."

"Our bond will always remain strong" Lythari promised the Queen.

Then, with a grateful look at Her Majesty and Aria, the two of them left the kingdom of Merland. Finley was waiting for them outside the gate. After expressing their heartfelt gratitude, they bid him farewell, and ascended into the night sky.

EIGHT

ART CAMP

The next day, Timmy woke up to a typical morning. There was nothing extraordinary about it, unless…

Timmy's gaze fell upon something unexpected. On his bedside table lay an extremely delicate shell-pendant, identical to the one Queen Calypso had gifted him in his dream.

He was stunned. He picked up the pendant, and its delicate curves and shimmering mother-of-pearl evoked memories of Merland. He rubbed his eyes, wondering if he was still dreaming.

No. The pendant remained, tangible and real.

Excitement mixed with trepidation.

How did it get here?

Is Merland real?

Is the pendant really from the Queen of the Merfolk?

Timmy's mind whirled with questions. He carefully hid the pendant in his top drawer, wrapped in a soft cloth. Only he knew its significance, and he believed it was real.

He did not try to push his thoughts. Sometimes, it was better to leave things undiscovered. Knowing it all would make it less fun. He looked at the mirror and smiled, and then got up to get ready for school.

At school, Timmy's thoughts drifted to the pendant and to Merland.

Emma noticed his distraction. "Hey, everything okay?"

Timmy hesitated, unsure how much to tell Emma. Nothing escapes the eyes of this girl, he thought to himself, "if only she was social beyond our friendship and put as much energy in school work as she does in playing detective over my body language, she would be more popular than me", his mind spoke inside his head. But he respected her as she is and wanted to change nothing about her or their friendship. He cherished their bond.

But he did not want to lie to her again. "Just lost in thought" he replied, downplaying his excitement.

After school, Timmy rushed home, eager to examine the pendant again.

He unwrapped it, studying every detail. Intricate carvings, delicate patterns, the shimmering pearl, a message– A message! Timmy looked closely. The writing was so light and faded that he hadn't noticed it in the morning with his sleepy eyes. But now he saw the sentence, etched across four of the shells, with one word on each of them:

Remember

the

secrets

shared

For a moment he thought he was hallucinating. Then he felt like he might have a heart attack. This was no ordinary trinket. The message confirmed that it was, in fact, the one Queen Calypso had given to him.

Timmy hid the pendant in his journal, which he tucked away in his bookshelf. Only Lythari and he knew its true meaning. Again, Lythari's words echoed in his mind:

You're a special boy, Timmy. Don't let anybody convince you otherwise.

Friday afternoon, Timmy packed his backpack with excitement. Art Camp was here, and he was excited as always.

He bid farewell to his parents and boarded the camp bus. He was happy to see some familiar faces from his school who he had only ever talked to at last year's Art Camp.

He recognised Emily, a bookworm with a passion for poetry; Ben, a thrill-seeker with a love for photography; and Lily, a music enthusiast with a flair for dance. They recognised him as well, and soon they all engaged in lively chat about their favourite books and authors, summer plans and adventures, and their artistic inspirations and idols. They high fived each other.

Emily: "Okay let's talk hobbies. What do y'all like to do in your free time?"

Ben: "I love photography! I'm always on the lookout for cool shots, mostly in the nature."

Lily: "That's awesome! I'm more into music. I sing and play the guitar."

Timmy: "Whoa, that's amazing! I've always wanted to learn guitar."

Lily: "You definitely should! It's so fun. But also, what about you? What are your hobbies, Timmy?"

Timmy: "I love drawing and painting. And I'm really into fantasy and adventure stories."

Emily: "No way! I love reading fantasy novels! Who's your favourite author?"

Timmy: "Hmm, that's tough. I'd say Tolkien and C.S. Lewis."

Emily: "Yes! The Chronicles of Narnia are my favourite!"

Ben: "This is wonderful because I too have always had a fascination of photography in a fantasy setting. Maybe we can collaborate on an art project?"

Lily: "That's a great idea! We could create a whole world together."

Timmy: "That would be epic! Let's do it!"

Emily: "I'll start brainstorming story ideas right away. Ben can take photos in the nature, which we will make into fantasy lands, Lily can provide the background score, and Timmy can illustrate."

Lily: "We can call it 'The Mythic Realms'!"

Ben: "I love it!"

Timmy: "It sounds really good! I love Art Camp!"

All of them cheered.

Just like every year, Art Camp was nestled in a picturesque valley, surrounded by towering trees, a sparkling lake, and vibrant wildflowers. The campsite itself was a tranquil oasis, with grassy lawns, winding pathways, and colourful gardens.

At its heart stood the main lodge, a rustic wooden structure with a warm and inviting atmosphere, featuring large windows that offered breath-taking views of the surrounding landscape. Inside, the lodge boasted a cosy fireplace, comfortable seating areas, and well-stocked art supplies. Adjacent to the lodge lay the dining hall, kitchen, and counsellor quarters, while scattered throughout the campsite were canvas tent cabins for campers, art studios, and outdoor classrooms.

A short walk from the main lodge led to a serene lake with canoes and kayaks, a forest trail for hiking and exploration, and a clearing for outdoor art projects and inspiration. According to Timmy, the camp's natural beauty and peaceful atmosphere made it the perfect setting for creative expression and growth.

Upon arrival, they were greeted by their Camp Art teacher, Ms Rodriguez.

"Welcome, young artists! Are you ready to unleash your creativity?"

Everybody cheered and whistled. Timmy's heart filled with joy. "Finally. The place where I never feel alone or judged" he said to himself, and smiled.

NINE

ADVENTURES AT ART CAMP CONTINUES

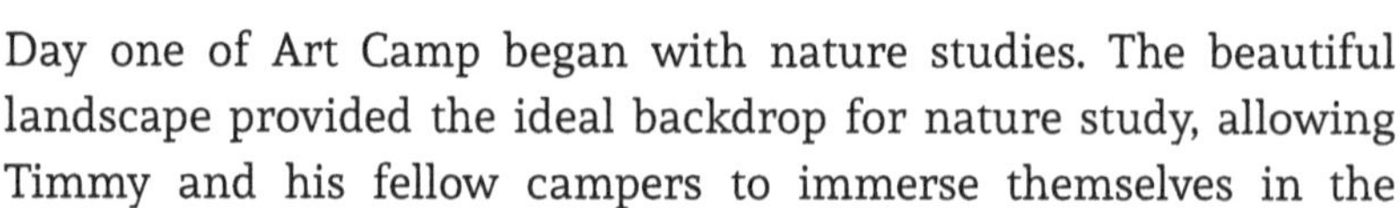

Day one of Art Camp began with nature studies. The beautiful landscape provided the ideal backdrop for nature study, allowing Timmy and his fellow campers to immerse themselves in the natural world.

The surrounding landscape, with its diverse flora and fauna, served as a living classroom, where they could observe and learn about the intricate details of nature. The forest trail, winding through towering trees and vibrant wildflowers, offered opportunities to study texture, colour, and pattern, while the serene lake allowed for observations of aquatic life and the interplay of light and water.

The camp's outdoor classrooms and clearing enabled hands-on exploration, where campers could collect leaves, rocks, and other natural materials to incorporate into their art. Through guided nature walks and independent exploration, Timmy and his friends developed a deeper appreciation for the natural world, honing their observation skills and learning to see the beauty in everyday details. As they sat by the campfire, sharing stories and sketches, the campsite's tranquil atmosphere fostered a sense of connection to the land, inspiring creativity and nurturing a lifelong love of nature.

Ms Rodriguez stood before the class, a warm smile on her face.

"Good morning, young artists! Today, we embark on an exciting journey through the world of watercolour."

She began by displaying a stunning watercolour piece. "Notice the soft blends, the vibrant colours, and the sense of movement."

"Watercolour is an ancient medium, modern watercolour painting originated in England in the mid-18th century, though history traces it back to the Palaeolithic era" she explained. Then she started discussing its unique characteristics.

Timmy learnt about watercolour's transparency, fluidity, and unpredictability, which Ms Rodriguez described as "embracing happy accidents."

She went on to demonstrate the various techniques of watercolour painting, including basic brushstrokes (flat, round, and filbert, colour mixing with primary, secondary and tertiary colours) and the wet-on-wet and wet-on-dry techniques, dropping tips and tricks here and there. "Use the white of the paper to your advantage," "Experiment with different brush angles," "Let the paint bleed and blend."

It was the most interesting and engaging class Timmy had ever attended. Everyone asked questions and shared observations.

"Wow, I never knew watercolour could be so versatile!"

"How do you achieve those soft edges?"

"What's the difference between hot and cold press paper?"

Ms Rodriguez answered each question, encouraging exploration and experimentation. When she concluded the lecture, the class felt inspired and eager to begin their watercolour journey.

"Remember the three P's – Practice, Patience and Playfulness," Ms Rodriguez reminded them. "And don't forget to embrace the unpredictability of watercolour."

The class nodded. With one final glance at the excited, wide-eyed faces, the teacher announced, "Alright now, I'll distribute the materials to each one of you, and then you'll begin your paintings for today. Let your creativity flow!"

As soon as the materials were distributed, the class dove into their first watercolour project. "A serene landscape with rolling hills and misty skies," Ms Rodriguez said. "And don't forget to give your painting a name."

Timmy's brush danced across the paper, colours blending and merging. He lost himself in the creative process, excitement building with each stroke.

His painting, which he decided to call "Sunset on the Lake" was a breath-taking watercolour piece that captured the serene beauty of the art camp's surroundings.

The composition featured a tranquil lake scene with the sun setting behind distant trees, soft feathery brushstrokes suggesting the gentle lapping of water against the shore, and a small wooden canoe partially hidden among the reeds adding a sense of human presence.

A warm colour palette dominated the sky, with oranges and yellows gradually deepening into hues of pink and purple, reflected in the surface of the lake with soft ripples and subtle texture. The surrounding foliage was painted in muted greens and browns, providing contrast to the vibrant sky.

Timmy employed the wet-on-wet technique to achieve soft blends and subtle texture, dry brush strokes adding depth and dimension to the trees and foliage, and a sprinkling of salt – which he had separately asked for from Ms Rodriguez – creating subtle speckled texture reminiscent of water droplets.

Delicate details included water lilies floating on the lake's surface and a small bird perched on a branch watching the sunset. Timmy left the edges of his painting rough and unfinished, giving the piece a sense of spontaneity.

Ms Rodriguez was stunned. Not only was Timmy's painting a stunning representation of the natural world but it also gave out a sense of invitation to the viewer to step into its serene atmosphere. She looked at it for two whole minutes, before saying, "Timmy, your attention to detail is remarkable. Your creativity knows no bounds." Timmy smiled. "Thank you, Ms Rodriguez."

The teacher lifted the painting slowly and carefully and then held it up for the entire class to see. The campers burst into an applause, some of them even whistled.

"Wow, Timmy, your drawing looks real!" they admired.

"Yeah Timmy, teach us your secrets!"

Timmy smiled sheepishly. This is exactly where I belong, he thought.

As the sun dipped below the horizon, the campers gathered around the crackling campfire, its warm glow illuminating their faces.

The evening air was filled with the sweet scent of s'more and the sound of laughter. Ms Rodriguez began the night's activities, sharing tales of famous artists and their inspirations, and sparking lively discussions among the campers.

Timmy and his friends eagerly shared their own artistic experiences, exchanging stories of triumph and frustration.

After their conversation was over, Ben pulled out his guitar, and started strumming a lively melody that had everyone clapping along. Lily joined in, her voice soaring as she sang a soulful rendition of a popular song. Emily recited an original poem, its poignant words captivating the audience. The campfire became a stage, with each camper showcasing their unique talents.

The night wore on. The group transitioned into a rousing game of "Would You Rather" sparking debates and giggles. "Would you rather have a lifetime supply of art supplies or be able to travel anywhere in the world?" sparked a heated discussion. The campers deliberated, weighing the pros and cons of each option.

Amidst the laughter and camaraderie, Timmy felt grateful for these new friendships forged in the creative crucible of art camp.

When the stars began to twinkle above, Ms Rodriguez distributed sparklers, their shimmering lights weaving a magical spell around the campsite. The campers took turns making wishes, their faces aglow with hope and optimism.

In this enchanted setting, the boundaries between reality and fantasy blurred, and the art camp became a world unto itself, where creativity and imagination knew no bounds. The night wore on, filled with s'mores, stories, and the sound of happy chatter, as the campers revelled in the joy of artistic expression and newfound friendships.

Day two of Art Camp brought with it new experiences. The campers eagerly boarded the bus, heading to the professional art studio of renowned artist, Mr Jenkins. Upon arrival, they were greeted by the artist himself, a warm smile on his face and twinkle in his eyes. Mr Jenkins welcomed them into his spacious studio, filled with natural light and the scent of oil paints. The room was a treasure trove of artistic expression, with canvases in various stages of completion, paint-splattered easels, and inspirational quotes adorning the walls.

He led them to his latest project, a stunning oil painting titled "Cosmic Dance." The piece depicted a swirling vortex of colours, evoking the birth of stars and galaxies. The campers gasped in awe, their eyes tracing the intricate brushstrokes and textures.

Timmy asked, "Mr Jenkins, how did you achieve this effect?"

"I used a combination of layering and glazing techniques to capture the depth and luminosity of the cosmos" the artist replied.

Emily inquired, "What inspires your artwork, Sir?" Mr Jenkins thought for a while. Then he said, "I find inspiration in the natural world – in the patterns, textures, and rhythms of nature. I try to capture its essence on canvas. You see, Nature never fails you, my friend." He winked at them.

Ben asked, "How long does it take to complete a piece?" Mr Jenkins chuckled. "It varies. Sometimes it takes months, even years, to bring a piece to life."

"Do you ever experience creative blocks?" Lily wondered. The artist smiled. "Yes, but I've learned to embrace them as opportunities to explore new techniques and perspectives." The campers nodded, exchanging looks of awe and admiration.

As they explored the studio, they discovered an array of Mr Jenkins' works, each one a testament to his mastery. "Aurora's Wings" featured delicate, feathery brushstrokes in shimmering hues of pink and gold; "Stellar Explosion" burst with vibrant colours, capturing the dynamic energy of a celestial event; while "Moonlit Serenade" whispered secrets of the night, with soft, ethereal lighting and gentle shadows.

Once they were done, Ms Rodriguez thanked Mr Jenkins for sharing his expertise and creative space. The campers departed, carrying with them inspiration, newfound knowledge, and the memory of an extraordinary encounter with a master artist. The visit had kindled a fire within them, fuelling their passion for art and creativity.

Ms Rodriguez turned to Timmy, her eyes shining with pride. "Timmy, I'd love for you to share your artwork with Mr Jenkins." Timmy's face flushed, but he nervously smiled, gathering his painting from the day before which he was asked by Ms Rodriguez to carry along, "just in case." Mr Jenkins, intrigued, walked over to Timmy. "Ah, Timmy, is it? Let's see what you've created" he said, grinning.

Timmy hesitated, then handed Mr Jenkins his painting, "Sunset on the Lake." He saw the artist's eyes widening as he took in the vibrant colours and delicate brushstrokes.

"Wow, Timmy, this is stunning!" Mr Jenkins exclaimed. "Your use of colour and light is remarkable. Do you have an inspiration?"

Timmy's voice trembled slightly. "I– I was inspired by the sunset at our Art camp. I tried to capture the feeling of peace and tranquillity of this place."

Mr Jenkins nodded thoughtfully. "You've succeeded beautifully. Your painting transports me to that serene lake shore. Your talent is undeniable."

The room fell silent, and Timmy could feel all eyes on him and his artwork.

Emily whispered, "Timmy, we're so proud of you." Ben and Lily nodded in agreement. Ms Rodriguez beamed. "Timmy, you've outdone yourself. Your hard work and dedication shine through."

Mr Jenkins continued, "Timmy, your artwork shows maturity beyond your years. Keep exploring, experimenting, and pushing boundaries. You have a bright future in the art world." The campers erupted into applause, and both the teacher and the artist joined them. Timmy's face glowed, his eyes shining with happiness.

"Th– thank you, Mr Jenkins, Ms Rodriguez" Timmy stammered, overwhelmed. "This means everything to me."

Ms Rodriguez wrapped a supportive arm around Timmy's shoulders. "You deserve every bit of this praise, Timmy." Everybody cheered in agreement. Mr Jenkins offered, "I'd like to display your painting in my studio's upcoming exhibition. Would you be interested?"

Timmy's jaw dropped. "Really? That would be incredible, Sir! I shall be honoured" he replied.

Ms Rodriguez smiled. "I think we have a budding artist on our hands."

The room filled with congratulations and encouragement, Timmy basked in the glow of his accomplishment, his heart filled with gratitude and inspiration. As the camp concluded, he felt not only inspired and motivated but also grateful for the new friendships he had formed.

He realised there are few things in his life that give him as much pleasure as painting, and was eager to explore his creativity and imagination even more.

The next day, with smiling faces and slightly heavy hearts, the campers boarded the bus to return.

The ride home was filled with the buzz of excitement and camaraderie, and some emotional moments as they hugged each other and talked about meeting again next year. Then, still high on the praise from Mr Jenkins, they all surrounded Timmy, eager to relive the moment.

Emily leaned in; her eyes were sparkling. "Timmy, you must share with us the *actual* inspiration behind your creativity?"

Ben chimed in, "Yeah, dude, you're a genius! It can't just be nature. I feel like you're hiding a secret." He looked at the others for support.

"Yeah, come on, confess! What's your magic formula?" Lily asked playfully.

Timmy's face flushed, his mind racing. He had never felt such admiration and such pressure to reveal his secret. Lythari's existence, hidden for so long, threatened to surface.

He took a deep breath, carefully crafting his response. "It's just my imagination, I assure you" he said, then seeing their unconvinced looks, quickly added, "And being around all of you, learning from each other. That too." A small voice inside appreciated , " good Timmy, you're learning useful social skills beyond just your fantasy world"... it sounded so much like Lythari's.

His fellow campers were not convinced, but Ms Rodriguez, seated nearby, smiled knowingly. "He's being modest. His talent and dedication are really praiseworthy." Although Timmy felt extremely shy, he was glad the teacher said this because the topic was dropped thereafter and everybody went back to other conversations regarding future art projects and collaborations. He found himself swept up in the excitement, his creative energy reignited.

Emily suggested, "We should start an Art club at school!"

"Yeah, and also that project that we'd planned to do. We must do that sometime soon!" Ben added enthusiastically.

Timmy's heart swelled, feeling part of a community that shared his passion. The bus pulled up to the camp drop-off point, marking the end of an unforgettable journey, they all hugged each other once more, and promised to speak more at school now that they were friends.

As Timmy stepped down, he knew his life had changed – his art, his friendships, and his connection to Lythari had forever intertwined.

On his way home, he realised that besides being full of joy and creativity, his heart was filled with another strong emotion – relief. Because even under stress, he'd managed to keep Lythari's secret safe with him. That is all that matters, he thought, as he walked home.

TEN

BEING CAUGHT AND BEING CHOSEN

Timmy burst through the front door, eager to share his art camp adventures with his mother. But instead of a warm smile, he was greeted by a stern stare on the couch.

He knew that face.

"Uh oh" he thought to himself! "Now, what have I done wrong?"

Even before his mother spoke, the pursed lips reduced to just a line, her big unblinking eyes and tense shoulders made a train of thought run in his mind "Did I forget some project due on Monday again?" "Did Grandma tell her anything about the dream stories I shared with her over video call Friday night". "Is she suspecting something?"

Broken from his reverie, Mrs Tint's stern voice pierced his thoughts "Where did you get this?" Mrs Tint asked, standing up and holding the shell pendant up for her son to see, her voice firm.

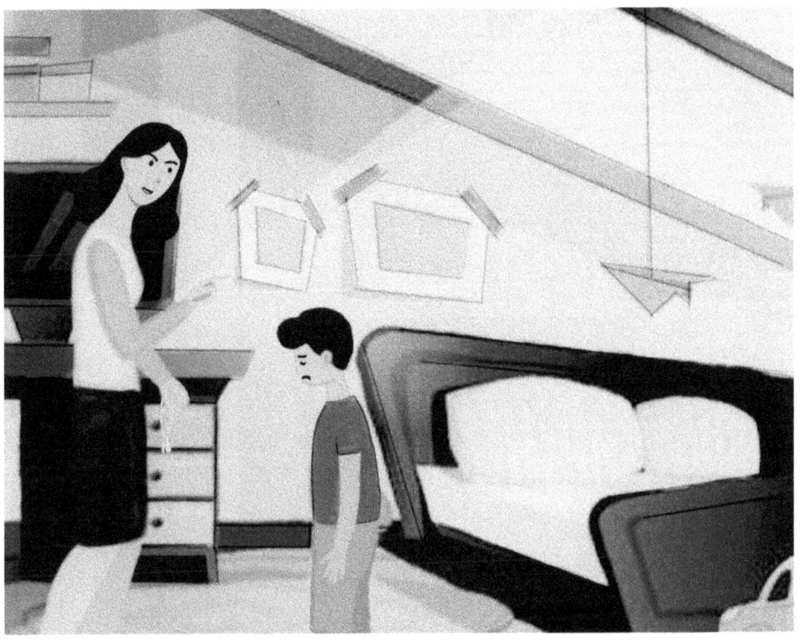

Timmy's excitement was replaced by unease. His mind racing to create a convincing lie, "Uh, I– found it on the beach, Mummy." He said smiling Sheepishly.

His mother's eyebrows narrowed and moved halfway up her forehead. "The beach? When?"

"During our last visit to Grandma's" Timmy muttered.

Mrs Tint's gaze intensified. "And what's this symbol on it?"

Timmy shrugged, feigning ignorance. "Just some weird marking, I guess."

Mrs Tint frowned. "Weird marking? Timmy, this looks like some sort of– *talisman*. What do you know about it?"

Timmy's heart raced, worried his mother would discover Lythari's existence. "Nothing, Mummy, I swear. I just found it lying on the beach and picked it up because I liked it."

Mrs Tint's voice softened slightly, but her concern remained. "Timmy, I want you to be honest with me. Is this connected to those drawings you've been making? or the stories from your dream you tell us since the last few years?"

Timmy hesitated, unsure how to respond. "No, Mummy. It's just a shell. Please don't worry about it. Ask Grandma, she knows."

"I want to trust you, but this feels off. Promise me you'll stay away from anything strange or unfamiliar" Mrs Tint responded, her eyes searching for the truth in her son's.

Timmy quickly nodded, eager to diffuse the tension. "Yes, I promise. I'll be careful" he said, as he saw his mother place the pendant on the kitchen counter, out of his reach. His heart sank. He realized he needed to be more cautious about protecting his connection to Lythari and his world.

"I'll keep this for now" Mrs Tint declared, looking back at her son with a questioning gaze. "If you found this at Grandma's, why didn't you tell me about it before?"

Timmy's mind raced, concocting a story. "Grandma and I– we had a secret. She told me to keep it just between us."

His mother raised one eyebrow. "A secret? What kind of a secret?"

"Grandma said it was a family tradition, passed down from her grandmother. She wanted me to have it, but asked me to keep it private" Timmy said, trying his best to sound convincing.

Mrs Tint's expression turned even more serious. "But you just said you found it on the beach."

Timmy felt his heart stop for a second. He raced his mind, trying to come up with an excuse. "I– I'm sorry, Mummy. I was trying to keep the secret."

His mother was visibly disappointed. "I'll ask Grandma about this the next time we visit. But why did you lie to me? This is not how I raised you" she said in a sad voice. Her pitch dropping. Creases on her forehead appeared.

Timmy's anxiety spiked, but he also felt bad for lying to his mother.

"Okay. And I'm really sorry, Mummy. I promise it won't happen again" he said, trying to be as calm as possible. He went forward and awkwardly Hugged her to make things look more normal.

Mrs Tint's gaze lingered on her son for a while, as if searching for any cracks in his story. "I know being honest all the time is not easy, and not everyone can be so. But remember that that's exactly what makes it the best. It always helps, darling" she said, and smiled kindly.

Timmy smiled back, relief washing over him as his mom dropped the subject. He felt safe, at least until their next visit to Grandma.

That night, Timmy drifted into a restless sleep, his mind still reeling from what happened in the evening. In his dream, he found himself standing on the familiar shores of Lythari's realm.

Lythari emerged from the mist, his eyes gleaming with sadness.

"Timmy, where were you?" Lythari asked, his voice tinged with hurt.

Timmy shifted uncomfortably, feeling guilty. "I was at Art camp. I didn't have time to visit, my naps were too short and infrequent."

Lythari's gaze intensified. "You didn't have time for me?" he asked in a whimpering voice, and hung his head low. "I waited. I always wait for you."

Timmy looked down, shamefaced. "I'm very sorry, Lythari. It's just...a lot happened."

Lythari's looked up, his eyes laced with concern. "What happened? You seem distant and distracted, my friend. Is everything all right?"

Timmy sighed, feeling the weight of his worries. "Mummy found the pendant. She's been questioning me."

"The pendant? Ah, the one from Queen Calypso. Yes, I feared this might happen" Lythari said gravely.

Timmy felt a surge of defensiveness. "It's not my fault! She just won't leave me alone."

Lythari's looked at him understandingly. "I know, Timmy. I've been sensing for a while that we're drifting apart. And I understand.

It takes a lot to recognise what you're feeling, and I'm proud that you do. That is the first step towards healing."

Timmy's gaze dropped. He knew Lythari was speaking the truth. "I'm tired, Lythari. I just want to sleep."

"Yes, I think you should. We'll keep today's quest on the hold, because now you need some rest" Lythari's kind voice whispered. "But I want you to promise me that you'll not let the outside world weaken our bond" he added.

Timmy nodded. "I promise, Lythari." As the dream faded, he felt a pang of regret for letting Lythari down. But exhaustion and stress consumed him, and he let sleep claim him once more.

The next day at school, the principal's voice boomed in the school's intercom, announcing the annual Inter-school Festival. Timmy's eyes widened as he heard his name being called out.

"...and representing our school in the Painting competition, we have Timmy Tint from fifth grade!"

The classroom erupted into applause, Timmy's friends cheering and whistling.

Emma high-fived him, then hugged him tightly. "Oh my god, Timmy! Congratulations!" She bounced up and down with joy. Timmy laughed. "You're going to do awesome!" she affirmed him.

Olivia rushed over to give Timmy a high-five. "Dude, you're a superstar! No one from our grade has ever been chosen in this category!"

Max chimed in, "We're so happy for you, Timmy!"

Timmy's face glowed with excitement. He, who probably had the fewest friends in his class, representing his school? He couldn't believe his ears.

The announcement continued. The class once again exploded with cheers as Mrs Thompson announced, "Olivia Hadley and Emma Mathews from fifth grade have been chosen as the representatives for the Poetry Reciting competition!"

Timmy and Emma hugged again, and Timmy patted her back. The other students whistled, then, realising the teacher was still in class, the chaos subsided.

Mrs Johnson beamed with pride. She congratulated Emma and Olivia, both of whom looked like they would burst into tears any moment.

Then she turned to Timmy. "See? I knew you had a gift for painting. Your drawings are exceptional!" Timmy thanked her. "This is a remarkable achievement," she continued. "This means you'll be competing against students from the higher grades."

At this, Timmy grew a little nervous, but his friends reassured him.

"You got this, Timmy!" Emma said, placing her hand upon Timmy's. "Yeah, thanks Emma. You too" he replied warmly.

"Yes, don't worry, we'll help you two figure it out," Olivia offered. "You should draw your favourite animal, Timmy!" she suggested.

Then, remembering that she had been chosen too, added, "Oh God, I have my own thing to prepare as well! What do you guys think, should I recite something original or a poem by my favourite poet?"

"I'd say don't risk it. Go for your favourite poet" Max said pulling her leg, and they all gave out a hearty laugh. Subsequently, they engaged in a serious discussion about what the three of them could do to win in their respective competitions. Timmy listened, his heart brimming with gratitude.

ELEVEN

THE ADDICTION OF ACHIEVEMENT

Back at home, Timmy shared the news with his parents as his heart swelled in joy. Mr and Mrs Tint exchanged a proud glance, but their smiles seemed tinged with concern.

"That's amazing, sweetie!" Mrs Tint said, hugging him tightly.

Mr Tint ruffled his hair. "Proud beyond words" he said.

But as they sat down to discuss the details, Timmy sensed something was wrong. Over the years, besides his creativity and ingenuity, Timmy had developed another talent worth noting, and this, he had learned by being with Emma who was Queen of the same. Sensing energies, shift in body language and facial expressions, even the most subtle change in tone of voice.

"What's wrong?" he asked.

His mother sighed. "We called Grandma today...about the pendant."

Timmy's heart skipped a beat. Almost choking on his own saliva. "And?" he pressed, trying to sound nonchalant.

Mr Tint cleared his throat. "She doesn't remember anything about it."

Timmy's mind raced. "Oh, but I do. Maybe she's just forgetful, you know, she's getting old" he said quickly.

His parents exchanged a concerning look. Timmy, feeling cornered, shifted gears. "You're not even happy about my Art camp or the contest! You're always worried about something else!" He burst into tears, stamping his foot and clenching his small fists at his sides. "You don't care about me! You only care about that stupid pendant!" His voice rose to a shriek, echoing through the room.

Mrs Tint tried to calm him down, "Timmy, sweetie, that's not true!"

But he wouldn't listen. He threw himself onto the floor, kicking his legs and flailing his arms. "I hate it! I hate it when you're always questioning me!"

Mr Tint knelt beside him, attempting to soothe his son. "No, son. We're extremely proud of you. Your Mummy and I love you a lot."

But Timmy continued to wail, his body shaking with sobs. He pounded his fists on the floor, his face red and tear-stained.

"Why can't you just leave me alone? Why can't you just be happy for me?" As he said these things, Timmy realised deep inside that he wasn't doing this just to get away with his lie, but that he had had these feelings bottled up inside him for a long time.

His mother gently stroked his hair. "We are happy for you, Timmy. We just want to understand what's going on, that's it."

Timmy's tantrum slowly subsided, replaced by hiccupping sobs. Mr Tint lifted him onto the couch, and Mrs Tint hugged him tightly as he cried himself out.

Once the storm had passed, Timmy's exhaustion took over, his eyelids drooping. His parents tucked him into bed, their faces full of concern and love.

"We love you. You're our darling boy," his mother whispered, smiling kindly at him. His father kissed his forehead. "Yes, no more questioning. Sleep tight, buddy."

But Timmy's dreams were already slipping into darkness, where Lythari's solemn face awaited him.

"Timmy, your pride is consuming you" Lythari said, his voice stern.

Timmy bristled. "I'm just happy about my accomplishments" he said, but he could already feel the shame engulfing him.

Lythari's gaze intensified. "Your creativity is your originality, Timmy. But of late you've been using your creativity to conjure up lies, and I don't like that. You're forgetting that our connection is based on honesty and purity of heart. Yes, I asked you to protect my secret, but not at the cost of lying to your parents and making them feel guilty about being worried for you."

Lythari's words pierced Timmy's defences. "No, Lythari! My art is mine alone!" he cried, defiance etched on his face. "I'm not forgetting anything! I'm just happy about my accomplishments."

"There's nothing wrong with that. But when your accomplishments get tainted by your ego, you no longer create for the joy of it, but for recognition."

Timmy's voice rose. "That's not true! I love art, and I *am* good at it."

Lythari's voice remained calm, but his words cut deep. "I think you're forgetting, dear friend, that most of your creativity is my gift to you. It stems from all the adventures we do together. And you're misusing my gift."

Timmy refused to accept it. "No, I don't believe that. I worked hard for my art."

Lythari sighed, his eyes filled with sorrow. "Of course you did, I never said you didn't. All I'm saying is that you're losing yourself. Your heart is no longer pure."

"You're just jealous! You're jealous of my success, because you aren't getting any recognition yourself" Timmy shot back, anger and frustration boiling over.

Lythari's face fell, and he looked wounded. "How can you say that, Timmy? I've always been there for you. And you know how happy I am about each of your achievements."

Timmy stood firm. Childlike tantrum had overcome his mask of maturity today. Exhaustion spoke on his behalf "You're always criticizing me, always telling me what to do. I don't need you." Pouting tearfully, sounding more like a five year old than himself.

"You're being rude, my friend. And you're breaking my heart. True friendship is precious, Timmy. Don't let ambition blind you" Lythari whispered, barely audible.

The argument hung in the air, a palpable tension between them. At these words, Timmy wavered, his resolve cracking.

But what Lythari said next shattered the momentary truce. "Perhaps it's time for me to leave. All these problems in your life, these lies, arguments, wouldn't have happened if not for me. I think it's for the best. Goodbye, dear Timmy" the Angel said, and before Timmy could say a word, vanished.

Timmy's eyes snapped open, his heart racing. He found himself lying on his side on the bed, clutching his pillow and sweating profusely. His heart beating loudly in his ears and eyes teary. He stared at the ceiling, gasping for air to calm himself down.

Lythari's words lingered, echoing in his mind like a threat. He felt helpless. What would he do without Lythari!

He was not ready to let this phase end, nor to navigate reality alone. He knew he had Mummy, Daddy, Grandma and Emma beside him, but he wasn't ready to not have Lythari, Not have the dream adventures.

Had he gone too far with his words?... Why was he defending himself before Lythari?... He could have told him the truth, what he actually felt, which was that Lythari was right about everything he said. He wouldn't have judged Timmy. Then why did he lie to him as well?... Was it developing into a habit now?... But then what else could he have done? Lythari was scolding him for lying to his parents, yet Lythari was the one who had told him to keep his identity a secret. He had no choice but to lie... Had Lythari left him for good? Was he never coming back?... Maybe it was for the best, as the Angel had himself said...

All these thoughts raced across his mind, and he stayed awake for the rest of the night. Tossing and turning.

Over the next few weeks, Timmy's behaviour underwent a drastic change. His love for art and creativity slowly withered away, and was replaced by an insatiable hunger for recognition and achievement.

At school, Timmy began to boast about his selection in the painting contest, constantly seeking validation from his classmates. He had always been popular among teachers but absolutely friendless except Emma , Max and Olivia. His art camp Friends were from a different grade and refused to openly acknowledge their friendship at school because Timmy was a well-known Weirdo at their grade, they didn't have the courage to fight that. This was the first time Timmy was being accepted and recognised by his classmates and Boy did it feel good finally. This was his chance to end being bullied.

"Do you know that I'm the youngest participant ever to be chosen for this category of the event?" he'd say, his voice dripping with pride.

"Wow, Timmy, you're so talented!" his classmates would respond, trying to appease him.

But his need for admiration knew no bounds. He started to dominate class discussions, interrupting others to share his own accomplishments.

Miss Johnson noticed this sudden change of attitude. She grew concerned. "Timmy, let others share their thoughts, too."

But Timmy wouldn't listen.

One day, during Art class, Emma showed him her latest painting. Timmy barely glanced at it, and then launched into a lengthy description of his own artwork. Emma's eyes drooped, her enthusiasm dampened. "That's nice, Timmy" she said in a quiet voice. Timmy ignored the sadness in her tone. He was already busy planning his next move and calculating how to win the contest.

His parents noticed this change as well. His room, once filled with colourful artwork, now displayed his trophies and certificates from different Art contests on the study table, which were previously kept with care in the glass showcase beside his closet. They covered some of his paintings that his father had hung up on the wall behind, and now all one could see on entering Timmy's room were his material achievements.

"Honey, what's happening with you?" Mrs Tint asked, overcome with worry.

Timmy shrugged. "I just want to be the best, Mummy, and I have a feeling I'm almost there."

His dreams, once vivid with adventures and hearty talks Lythari, now grew shallow and infrequent. Lythari's presence faded into the background, replaced by visions of victory and applause.

One night, he had a dream where he stood on stage accepting the first prize in something, while the crowd cheered, whistled and applauded for him. But then–

Timmy woke up with a start, his heart pounding. He felt he had seen something in the dream that he hadn't seen for a while.

Did I dream of Lythari? he wondered. But the memory was hazy, and soon the thought too got lost in the haze of his ambition. Who cares, I just dreamt of winning, he thought, and drifted back to sleep.

As the Inter-school fest approached, Timmy's obsession with winning intensified. He spent every waking moment practising and perfecting his craft.

Amidst all the chaos, a small voice occasionally whispered in his mind, "What about Lythari? What about their adventures? What of the joy of creation? Is winning all that matters now?" But Timmy silenced it, focusing on the prize.

His obsession with winning the contest consumed him, driving him to focus solely on the technical aspects of art. He spent hours studying the works of famous artists, analysing their brushstrokes, colour palettes, and compositions.

He began to replicate their masterpieces, painstakingly recreating every detail and sacrificing his originality and imagination in the process. I want to leave no stone unturned, he said determinedly to himself.

Miss Lawrence noticed the change in his approach. "Timmy, where's the originality in your drawings? Your unique voice was what made them so appreciable, and now it feels like your paintings have deteriorated. Why do you suddenly feel the need of recreating already-famous paintings?"

Timmy shrugged. "I'm just trying to improve my skills, Miss. But I'll try to hold on to my own imagination from now on" he said. But deep down, he knew he was losing his creative spark.

One day, in the English class, Emma confronted him. "Timmy, your art used to be so full of life! Now it's just...copies. I miss your old paintings." She puckered her face childishly as usual, sounding dramatically grumpy, Timmy felt annoyed at her innocence which he mistook to be lack of awareness about the world.

Timmy's defence mechanism kicked in. "These are masterpieces, Emma! I'm learning from the best. You know nothing about art. I think you should focus on the Poetry competition instead of worrying about me."

Emma ignored the hurtful remark as if it didn't even reach her ears. "But what about your own style? Your own story? All those adventures with– what was the name– ah, Lythari, right? What about those?" she said tiptoeing and pressing on the desk with her arms, shaking it slightly.

Lythari's name struck Timmy like a jolt of lightning. "That was just kids' stuff. I need to grow now as an artist, Emma, and I have a feeling I already am. Now if you'll excuse me," he said dismissively, and shifted to Olivia's desk next to theirs, since she was absent that day. Emma's heart sank, but she knew he will turn around in no time. So she decided against calling him back. Also Emma was another wonder who didn't know how to remain sad, she was always fluttering, even though she deeply cared.

Timmy delved deeper into technicality, neglecting the emotional connection that once drove his creativity. Lythari's absence grew more pronounced, his guidance and inspiration silenced by Timmy's ego.

One day, while trying to replicate Van Gogh's *Starry Night*, he noticed how mechanically his hand moved, and how numb his mind had gone. Suddenly, he felt a pang of emptiness.

Is this really art? he wondered.

But, like always, the doubt was fleeting, and soon it was crushed by his determination to win. As the fest drew near, Timmy's portfolio overflowed with replicas of famous paintings that were technically flawless, yet soulless to their core.

His heart, once full of passion and creativity, had become a hollow vessel, filled with echoes of others' genius.

TWELVE
THE ANNUAL FEST

The day of the annual festival finally arrived, and Timmy's school was abuzz with excitement since theirs was the one hosting it. Students and guardians filled in the school auditorium.

The fest was called *Creativity Unleashed*, and it showcased the artistic talents of students from various schools. The venue was transformed into a vibrant auditorium, with colourful streamers and balloons adorning the walls.

The fest commenced with the Dance competition, 'RhythmsofLife', where the audience was greeted by a mesmerizing dance performance by a group of senior students from the host school. The music began, a fusion of classical and contemporary beats, and the dancers started moving in synchronized steps as they swayed to the beats, their feet tapping out a lively rhythm.

The lead dancer, a graceful girl with flowing hair, spun and leaped across the stage. Her movements were fluid, like a river flowing effortlessly. The others joined in, forming intricate patterns with their bodies. The audience watched, entranced, as the music shifted to a melancholic tune, and their movements slowed. Then the rhythm picked up again, and the energy on-stage soared, matching the beats of the song. The performance concluded with a thunderous applause, and the dancers took their well-deserved bows.

The emcee announced, "And that was 'RhythmsofLife' from *The Dynamic Steppers!*"

The audience cheered, whistling and clapping along. Timmy clapped, his eyes wide with wonder.

For a moment, he forgot about the painting contest and let the beauty of the performance wash over him.

He recalled how Lythari, during one of their quests, had told him, "Never let your sense of self consume you so much that you forget to appreciate the creativity around you." He almost smiled, but then remembered. "No", he thought, "I can't let Lythari distract me again." The moment passed, and his focus returned to his own event, that would commence soon.

One by one, participants from the three other schools took over the stage, clad in vibrant costumes. All their performances were met with significant applause and appreciation from the judges.

The next event was Poetry Slam, and it was named 'Poetry Punch' where the participants were required to recite a poem, original or borrowed.

The auditorium got busy as people shifted in their seats, and the judges of the Dance competition got up to make space for the new judges.

Then the emcee arrived on stage, and Emma's was the first name to be called out. She stood up from her seat, two rows ahead of where Timmy was sitting, and he noticed that she had saved a seat beside her. She turned around, as if searching for someone. Her eyes briefly met Timmy's, and she smiled at him nervously. Timmy smiled back, and put both his thumbs up in the air for her to see. She gave a soft laugh and nodded, then walked to the stage. He's turned back around to his usual self, she sensed with relief.

She took her place at the microphone, her hands trembling slightly.

The judges smiled encouragingly. "Go ahead, dear" said one of them.

With one final glance at Timmy, she closed her eyes, cleared her throat, and began:

"Two paths crossed, two hearts entwined,

In laughter and tears, we've shared our time.

Timmy, my friend, my partner in crime,

Together we've danced, in sunshine and rhyme.

Your brushstrokes bring colour to my day,

My words weave tales to drive your imagination's sway.

In dreams, you've soared, on eagle's wings,

In reality, our bond remains, unbroken strings.

Through thick and thin, through joy and fear,

Our friendship stands, year after year.
With every step, with every fall,
We'll lift each other up, through it all.
Timmy, my friend, my shining star,
Forever in my heart, near and far."

Emma finished reciting her poem, and opened her eyes. Blushing .The first person they landed on was Timmy, who was staring at her, and his face looked like he was in shock, appreciation, understanding, friendship and embarrassment all playing at the same time. "Oh no Emma is too innocent" he thought. "Now the bullies will bully me more and call us a couple." "why did she have to read this aloud" " nobody will understand our friendship, she still thinks things are as simple as things were back in nursery days". But quickly he brushed aside the thoughts as appreciation and wonder and gratitude washed over.

Emma smiled. Both of them realised how distant they had gotten from each other in the past few weeks. For a second, there was nobody else in the auditorium, but just them, giving each other a look of understanding. This lasted for five brief seconds, and then the audience erupted into applause, moved by her heartfelt poem. Emma started back to the present moment, and saw the judges smiling, impressed by her performance. Then she saw a group amongst the audience standing up, and within seconds found herself receiving a standing ovation from her small group of close friends, followed by a special mention from the judges, for her originality and heartfelt content. She bowed, thanked everyone, and exited the stage, as her parents and friends patted her shoulder and cheered for her once more.

Timmy's eyes welled up with tears, touched by what had just happened. Emma had written and recited a poem solely for him, even though she knew the others would recite poems by great poets and probably win. He felt a pang of regret for neglecting their friendship lately. Suddenly, Lythari's words came to his mind. *True friendship is precious, Timmy. Don't let ambition blind you.*

Without a second thought, he got up from his seat and rushed over to hug his best friend. As he was walking down, the emcee called Olivia's name for the next performance. Olivia got up from his seat and Timmy almost stumbled into her. "All the best, Olivia!" he murmured, to which she smiled and thanked him. Emma and Max, too, wished her luck, and she ran up to the stage in excitement.

Once she had left, Timmy went up to Emma. "That was amazing!" he exclaimed.

Emma's eyes, too, filled with tears. "Thanks, Timmy. I wrote it for you" she said, rubbing her eyes.

On the stage, Olivia was reciting a poem by Robert Frost, and Timmy and Emma listened to her while conversing.

"Yeah, I figured. You took my name like ten times," Timmy joked, and Max laughed out loud from the seat next to Olivia's. Emma smiled sheepishly, and gave him a light push on the chest. "You mind if I sit here?" Timmy asked, pointing at the empty seat beside her.

Her smile grew wider, and she shook her head.

Timmy realised at that moment, he had been so busy hogging all the attention himself, that he never truly appreciated or realised Emma for who she was growing up to be, she was becoming her own person beyond the tiny bubbly rabbit like dramatic little girl.

He sat down, and the two of them listened attentively as Olivia finished reciting the poem. There was a huge round of applause from everyone in the auditorium, irrespective of which school they were supporting. Timmy and Emma looked at each other and smiled proudly.

In that moment, Timmy felt that their friendship, forged through laughter and tears, shone brighter than any contest or achievement.

The 'Culinary Delights' cooking competition showcased the culinary talents of students, with innovative dishes that wowed the judges and the audience equally well.

One notable creation was the "Saffron Sunset" a stunning dessert featuring saffron-infused crème brûlée, topped with a vibrant orange-ginger glaze and edible flowers, prepared by a student of their neighbouring school.

Another standout was the "Spicy Taco Tornado" where a group of senior students from Timmy's school created a unique taco shell made from crispy plantain chips, filled with spicy shrimp, avocado, and sour cream.

Meanwhile, another student combined Indian and Italian flavours to present what he called the "Bombay-Italian fusion" a delectable chicken tikka lasagna with cardamom-infused béchamel sauce.

The creativity continued with "Rainbow Sushi" – colourful sushi rolls crafted using natural food dyes and filled with creative ingredients like strawberry-basil and crab-mango.

However, Timmy's favourite to look at was the "Chocolate Chai Cake," a moist chocolate cake infused with the warmth of tea spices and topped with a creamy cardamom frosting, and for a moment he wished he were one of the judges just so he could taste it.

The other impressive dishes included the "Japanese-style Ramen Burger" featuring a juicy pork patty sandwiched between ramen noodle "buns" and topped with pickled ginger and wasabi mayo, the "Frenchie Falafel" that gave the classic falafel a French twist by serving crispy falafel balls in a flaky croissant with creamy hummus and pickled vegetables, and the "Tropical Tarts" miniature key lime and mango tarts garnished with edible flowers and micro greens.

The innovative dishes impressed the taste buds of the judges, showcasing the creativity and culinary skills of the student chefs.

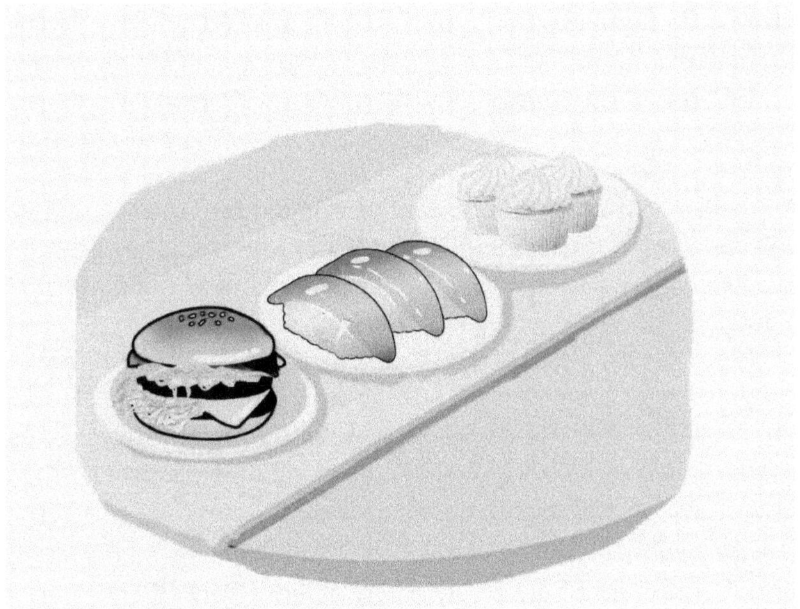

Timmy's event was the last one for the day. The painting competition was called "Brushstrokes of the Genius."

As Timmy walked onto the stage, he heard a few gasps in the audience. "He's too small to compete with all these senior students" one senior from a different school was saying.

"Yeah, at least Emma Mathews and Olivia Hadely went against students their age, but this category always has senior students. What was the school even thinking?" another remarked.

Timmy's confidence faltered a little, but he was determined. The topic was announced. It was "Nature's Wonders" and participants had two hours to create their pieces.

As Timmy gathered his materials, his minds shuffled through the various competitions that he had seen unfold since morning. He recalled how each participant poured their passion and soul into their craft, transcending technical perfection.

He thought of Emma's poem, and how it had touched his heart. Her words came rushing to him, and he was reminded of the joy they shared through art.

He began to question his obsession with technicality. Was it truly worth losing the essence of his creativity for the genius of some famous painter? he thought.

Suddenly Timmy felt a surge of determination. He would not let his obsession with winning consume him. He would create from the heart. With a deep breath, he began drawing. His brushstrokes loosened, and colours merged in a beautiful dance.

His artwork, which he called "The Guardian of the Forest" brimmed with his creativity, infused with a new sense of life and emotion. The tree's branches swayed with a gentle elegance, its leaves shimmering with dew. In the middle of the forest stood Lythari, his eyes sparkling with curiosity, as fireflies danced about him in abandonment. As he gave the finishing touches, Timmy felt as if he had rediscovered his own soul through this painting.

THIRTEEN

RESULTS

Once they were all done, the emcee asked them to hold up their paintings for everyone to see. The judges' comments and the audience's applause faded into the background as Timmy held his up, his heart telling him he had created something true to himself. A deep inhalation of relief mingled with paint-stained fingers, as Timmy realized he had broken free from the shackles of perfection. Art, once again, had become the extension of his soul.

The audience watched all the paintings in awe, and some of them discussed amongst themselves which one was going to win the competition.

The judges deliberated, scrutinizing each artwork, and then jotted down the scores on their respective boards.

Meanwhile the students explored the games stalls and food carts, joined by their guardians who were till now seated in a formal seating arrangement in one side of the auditorium . Max almost broke the record at the "shoot the balloons" game and won a stuffed unicorn which he handed over to his little brother who too had come alongside his parents. Timmy wanted to go on the bouncy castle but decided against it. "I'm already bullied enough for my eccentric imagination, now Emma's recitation, I definitely do not want the jocks to notice me wobbling on the bouncy castle" he thought to himself, but deep down he wanted to be on it.

Suddenly Olivia emerged from behind one of the food carts carrying huge buckets of fried chicken. "Guys! These are not the Olympics. Why the seriousness? Let's have some fun! When was the last time you ate today Timmy?

Her mother joined in "yes, kids, remember the main objective of this fest is to explore and have fun, more, to bond, winning or losing is not even secondary, its tertiary".

Max's Dad added, "yes eat, you all will miss this once you grow up".

"Thank God their school allows parents at the event, so we too can get a taste back of our childhood" Timmy's father joined in.

They all chuckled and chatted for another few minutes while the children snacked on fried chicken wings and fresh juices happily. They have been very hungry. After all it was a long event.

After they finished the food Emma pulled Timmy by one hand and Olivia by the other to participate in more games, " ring the toy" , "break the pot", "fortune telling" and most interestingly , "water cannon ball" in which a volunteer was getting dunked in a pool every time they hit the target with the ball to be thrown with one hand.

The break lasted for an hour in total, while the results would be announced back inside the auditorium, the now bustling with activity playground would wrap up and return to the usual , waiting yet another year to turn into a carousel of a fairground.

As the bell sounded, the students streamed in one line to enter their designated seating area while the parents gently and gracefully took theirs seat at the other half of the auditorium.

After everyone got seated and silence was regained, finally, it was time for the results.

The emcee called out the names of each category one by one and the participants gathered on stage.

The auditorium burst into applause and whistles as the senior girls' team from Timmy's school won the dance competition.

Next up was the singing competition, which Timmy had missed, since he had gone to gather his art equipment. This was won by one of the other competing schools, and everybody clapped, the excitement slightly lower than before.

Not for long, though, since following this were the results of the Poetry Slam, and for a second it seemed like there was an explosion in the auditorium as the emcee read out, "The winner of Poetry Slam is Olivia Hadley from Winter Dale School for her brilliant recitation of "Design!"

But he didn't stop there. "And a special mention from the judges to Emma Mathews from Winter Dale School for her courage, certitude and creativity to read aloud her own original composition .It was an outstanding gesture!" Timmy and all his classmates stood up to clap for the two of them, and Emma, who had never ever participated with the thought of winning, now jumped up from her seat in excitement for both herself and Olivia, her usual unique fluttering in joy and innocence style.

Olivia gave out a loud shriek, and rushed to the stage to collect her prize. Timmy was very happy for them.

Everybody clapped and cheered as the winner of culinary delights, though from another school, the maker of the "Chocolate Chai Cake," ascended the stairs to the stage. "Very well-deserved, it looked extremely tasty," Timmy heard one of his peers say.

"I called it" said Timmy, as he smiled and applauded.

His excitement gradually gave way to anxiety as it was now time for the results of the painting competition to be announced. Emma looked at him and nudged light-heartedly; assuring him that everybody in the audience thinks it'll be him. Timmy felt a surge of happiness, and waited on his toes as the emcee collected the final markings from the judges.

"The winner of the Inter-school painting competition "Brushstrokes of the Genius" is–"

Timmy almost stood up. He hoped it was going to be him.

"–Oliver Russell from Blue Bright International School!"

The audience erupted into applause, as the students from Timmy's school groaned.

Timmy felt as if the floor had slipped from beneath his feet, and he would fall anytime. He wavered on his feet, half-standing, and Emma caught him by the arm. "You okay. Timmy?" He nodded. "It doesn't matter. You're the winner for us, for the audience." She smiled broadly, looking genuinely happy. But she was she. Even a colourful scented eraser found on the corridors lighted her up the same way. Timmy reflected, "Why can't I be so innately joyous like Emma?"

But he was him. Different. Creative. The dreamer. The recent achiever. He felt he had let down the entire school by not being able to keep up with his special nomination even though much young for the category.

"Yeah, Timmy. If there was an award for the fan favourite, that would be you!" Max interjected his train of thought and tried to cheer him up.

The winner was a high school student, and he had created a breath-taking landscape featuring some of the endangered species of wildlife. He ran to the stage, while Timmy sat back down, his face clouded with disappointment.

His sadness was palpable, but his parents beamed with pride. "You did amazing, Timmy!" Mrs Tint exclaimed from two rows behind him. "Yes, son. You did extremely well. It was beautiful" agreed Mr Tint next to her.

Timmy forced a smile at them, his heart heavy. Somewhere deep down, he did a feel a tinge of contentment, as he knew he had created from the heart. But he was very confused about these new emotions. All he knew was that at that moment, Lythari's absence felt more pronounced than ever. His mind wrestled with conflicting desires, torn between two aspects of himself.

On one hand, his dreamy creative self-yearned to soar on wings of imagination, finally letting go of the technicalities of art and the obsession with winning. This part of him revelled in the joy of creation, unbridled by criticism or expectation, and thanked Lythari's guidance that had nurtured this self, fostering a deep connection with his artistic soul.

On the other hand, however, he felt dreadful and embarrassed that he hadn't won. Had he really been able to completely let of the thought of winning? Surely not, since he felt terrible at his loss. The taste of pride, success, and appreciation had awakened a new craving within him. He craved the validation of others, the thrill of winning, and the recognition that came with it. This part of him recalled every brushstroke, scrutinizing in his mind what all could have gone wrong.

The contest had ignited this flame, and Timmy struggled to distinguish between genuine passion and external validation. Which one truly brought him joy?

He pondered. Was it the unbridled creativity of his dreamy self that manifested in his artwork, or were it the accolades of the world?

Emma's lines came to his mind, "Your brushstrokes bring colour to my day." He started analysing it in a negative light. Why did she say *his* brushstrokes bring colour to *her* life? Why not to his *own* life? Was his art for himself or others?

He looked up from his reverie at the stage where the winning painting was at display and at that very moment something happened to him. The beautiful creation was beyond marvellous, each brushstroke a perfect blend of originality, creativity and meticulous practice and technical mastering. He knew it was most just for this painting to win. He realised he had a long long way to go to reach this stage and at that realisation all the clouds lifted and he genuinely felt grateful for the lesson thus learned and happy for Oliver Wilson. Genuinely happy.

A smile of contentment and satisfaction crept up his face and he knew exactly why Emma was jumping up and down even after not winning after having recited her original poetry.

As he reflected, he looked around. The audience was gradually filing out of the auditorium. He saw the seat beside his was empty, and realised he hadn't noticed when Emma had got up to congratulate the winners. He saw her and Olivia posing with them in front of the stage for a picture together, smiling wide, Olivia holding up her trophy and Emma her certificate for the camera.

Further, a realization dawned on Timmy. He was being too critical of himself. His creative self and his desire for recognition were not two things mutually exclusive. And they didn't have to be. They could co-exist, balancing each other.

His dreamy self could thrive while still acknowledging the value of external appreciation. As soon as he thought this way, the fest results stopped mattering as much, since they no longer defined his worth as an artist. His inner turmoil subsided, replaced by harmony between his two selves.

With renewed clarity, Timmy understood that true joy came from embracing both aspects. He would create for himself, from the heart, while welcoming the world's recognition.

But for now, he should be happy for his friends, like he knew they would have been had he won. He got up from his seat with a wide smile on his face, and congratulated Emma and Olivia once again.

He also held out his hand for Oliver Russell to shake, but the young man ignored his hand and pulled him into a tight hug instead. "Yours was really beautiful, Timmy. My personal favourite" he winked at him. Timmy's heart grew, and he saw his parents smiling at him, looking proud.

Lythari's voice returned, and this time it was so loud Timmy felt as if he was standing right next to him. "See, Timmy? It takes nothing to be a good person. I'm so proud of you for navigating through your conflicting thoughts all by yourself and accepting the truth. You know what takes a lot? That. Remember to always listen to your heart, just how you did right now, and create from your soul. Recognition will follow automatically."

Timmy smiled. "And it's okay if it doesn't" he completed.

FOURTEEN
LYTHARI RETURNS

That night, as Timmy drifted off to sleep, he felt a familiar presence beside him that had long been missing. Lythari's gentle smile and soft shimmering eyes welcomed him back. They sat together on Timmy's terrace, this time in his dream, surrounded by the moonlit darkness.

"Congratulations, young artist" Lythari said, his voice warm with pride. "Your journey in these past few months has been remarkable. Almost made me wonder if I should leave more often" the Guardian joked.

Timmy's eyes sparkled with excitement. "Lythari! I missed you so much! Please never even think of leaving me again" he said, and hugged his dear friend.

Lythari's expression softened. "Ha-ha! I'm joking, Timmy. I never really left you, you know?"

Timmy looked up. "You– didn't?" he asked, confused.

"Nope. I've been with you, guiding you through your struggles. And boy was it difficult at first. You had too many negative thoughts and emotions in there."

Lythari pointed at Timmy's heart. "But then, slowly, your heart started cooperating, *you* started cooperating with me.

I couldn't have done it without your own help, and without you not wanting it to happen. So, when I say it was all you, Timmy, I mean it. I can only help those who *want* to be helped. And now I must say, you've grown immensely."

Timmy listened to these words with his eyes closed. When he opened them, he felt some big weight had lifted off his chest, and felt he was content and at peace with himself after a long time.

"I felt lost between my creative self and the desire for recognition" Timmy confessed.

Lythari nodded. "Now you've learned to balance both. Your art is a reflection of your unique soul, and sharing it with others enhances its beauty."

Timmy shared his experiences at Art camp and in karate classes, about the new techniques he had learnt and new friendships he had forged. Lythari listened attentively, offering words of affirmation and encouragement and occasionally cracking jokes to make his friend laugh whenever the topic got serious.

As the night deepened, their conversation delved into deeper emotional topics.

"Fear, self-doubt, and anxiety will be natural companions on your journey" Lythari said. "Embrace them, like you did today, and they will become your greatest teachers."

Timmy's eyes shone with understanding. "I see now. I was chasing perfection, and was afraid of not being the best."

Lythari's smile reassured him. "Perfection is an illusion, Timmy. I'm sure you know it by now. You don't have to be perfect, in fact, you never can. Nobody can. You know why? Because there *is* no such thing. All you have to be is enough, not for others, but for yourself, which you already are. Your uniqueness is your greatest strength."

Timmy smiled at him with eyes full of gratitude. "What would I have done without you Lythari" he said, and hugged his angelic friend once again.

"You would have done just fine" Lythari said, hugging him back and patting his head. Slowly but steadily, their conversation meandered through the realms of creativity, self-expression, and the importance of relationships.

As the first light of dawn crept over the horizon, Lythari stood up. Timmy was all too familiar with this "technique" now, and he followed suit, eagerly waiting for the Guardian to make the much-awaited announcement that he had not heard for months now.

With one look at Timmy, Lythari spread his wings as he stood, and declared, "It's time for our next great adventure."

Timmy was so happy to hear Lythari finally say it that he started jumping and clapping with joy. "Tell me, tell me Lythari! Where to shall be our next journey?"

Lythari's face broke into an enigmatic smile, hinting at wonders to come. "Tonight, we embark on a journey to the majestic Mount Everest" and before Timmy could register this information, the Guardian moved his wings in a circular motion and the brightest rays of light appeared creating a vortex of a portal in that dark night out of nowhere.

Timmy covered his eyes with his hands, but next moment, the light had vanished, and he looked up. He almost lost his balance at what he saw next. The Angel smiled at his half-puzzled, half-scared look, and clarified, "This is our portal for the night" then sensing that Timmy still had questions, said in a joking tone, "You didn't think we'd fly to a different continent altogether, did you? If it were just me, I would've done that in a pop– " he snapped his fingers "– but with you, it would take us months."

To this, Timmy laughed out loud. "Understandable" he said, and held Lythari's wing.

They stepped through the portal. Timmy felt a little dizzy as there seemed to be a sudden whirlwind around him, but it was momentary, and the next thing he knew, he was standing at the base of Mount Everest, still clutching Lythari's wing, who was looking up at the mountain peak as if they were two friends meeting after a long time.

"Ah," said the Angel, "So long, Everest, so long."

Timmy, shivering with cold, followed Lythari's gaze and looked up. It was daytime there, and he saw vividly the snow-capped peaks of the Himalayan range – that he had read about in his Geography book and that his father had pointed out to him on the globe – towering above, and spotted Everest standing tall amidst them like a

Queen, its grandeur awe-inspiring.

Timmy's jaw dropped. He had imagined seeing a lot of places with Lythari that were otherwise impossible for him to see, but – he admitted to himself – the highest mountain peak in the world was definitely not one of them.

Lythari handed him a pair of insulated boots and a warm parka. "Prepare for the climb" he instructed. Timmy could hardly speak, so he merely nodded, and took his position as the Guardian guided him.

They trekked through the icy terrain, their footsteps echoing in the stillness. Timmy felt as if with every step the air grew thinner, and his lungs worked harder. Lythari's calm voice was the only thing keeping him steady on the treacherous path.

As they kept ascending, the night with its engulfing darkness descended. Stars twinkled above, and everything around except for Lythari became invisible to Timmy.

Suddenly, a rustling sound came from a nearby cave. Timmy looked Lythari fearfully. "We have arrived, Timmy, turn around" he said.

Timmy's confusion gave away to fear and fascination as he saw turned around and saw a towering figure emerging from the shadows. His white fur glistened in the moonlight, and his eyes shone with ancient wisdom.

"The Yeti" Lythari informed, answering Timmy's awe and fear.

The Yeti came forward and knelt down beside Timmy, and Lythari introduced them. The humongous creature welcomed him with a gentle nod, then with hands as huge as a saw, gestured for them to follow him.

Timmy and Lythari did as they were told. The Yeti led them into his cave, where a warm fire crackled. Steam rose from cups of tea, and he offered one to each of his guests. Lythari gently shook his wings, while Timmy gratefully accepted.

After they were done drinking the tea, they delved into conversations about the mesmerising place. The Yeti shared tales of the mountain's secrets and the balance of nature. Timmy listened intently, absorbing the wisdom.

"Long ago," the ape-like wonder began to speak, "Everest was a sacred place, where the Gods dwelled. The mountain's snow-capped peak held the secrets of the universe. The ancient saints came to worship and seek guidance."

As he spoke, his eyes sparkled with a deep connection to the mountain.

"Balance is key," he continued. "Nature's harmony depends on respect and reciprocity. The wind whispers secrets to the trees. The rivers carry the memories of the land, and the creatures roam free, sharing a beautiful bond amongst themselves."

He then proceeded to tell them the stories of the mysterious creatures that inhabited the Himalayas. His large grey eyes sparkled as he shared the tale of Khansa, the snow leopard, who roamed the Himalayas with grace and stealth many many years ago, her fur blending seamlessly with the snow and making her nearly invisible.

Possessing ancient wisdom passed down through generations, Khansa knew the secrets of the mountain. During a harsh winter, a severe storm threatened the land, and the leopard ventured out, using her keen senses to locate a hidden spring, guiding the other creatures to safety and saving them from certain death. Recognizing her selflessness, the mountain spirits gifted her with the power to heal, and her presence could calm the fiercest storms and soothe troubled hearts.

The Yeti's gaze drifted into the distance as he concluded, "Khansa's legacy lives on, her spirit continues to protect and guide, and reminding us that respect and reciprocity are the keys to harmony." The tale faded into the crackling fire, leaving Timmy with a sense of wonders and awe for the majestic Khansa.

The Yeti began again, and his voice filled the cave as he recounted the tale of Tenzin, the magical red panda. "In the lush forests of the Himalayas, Tenzin lived a peaceful life, munching on bamboo shoots and berries. Her gentle nature and curious spirit made her a beloved friend to all creatures. One day, a devastating landslide destroyed her home, leaving Tenzin alone and frightened.

But she didn't fall in despair. Using her agility and quick thinking, she helped guide her fellow animals to safety, leading them to a hidden valley filled with abundant food and shelter. The mountain spirits, moved by her selflessness, gifted her with the power to communicate with all creatures, great and small.

From that day onwards, Tenzin roamed the mountains, spreading harmony and understanding wherever she went, reminding us that even in times of turmoil, compassion and kindness can prevail." The Yeti's eyes now shone with warmth, and Timmy's heart swelled with admiration for the courageous yet gentle red panda.

With each tale, Timmy felt the Yeti's deep love for the wilderness and the natural world. "The mountain's power is not to be conquered," the majestic creature cautioned. "Instead, listen to its whispers. Learn from its ancient wisdom. That would do humans some good."

As the night wore on, the Yeti went on to reveal his own story. His eyes clouded, his voice heavy with sorrow, as he began his tale. "Centuries ago, humans lived in harmony with the natural world, respecting the land, creatures, and elements. But over time, they grew selfish and forgot the old ways, seeking to conquer, dominate, and exploit. Their connection to the earth frayed, and the balance shifted. The forests shrank, rivers polluted, and creatures vanished. The wind still whispered secrets to the trees, but humans no longer listened. Rivers carried memories of the land, but humans forgot. Creatures roamed free, but humans saw them as mere resources and caged them."

His gaze drifted towards the flames, his voice barely above a whisper. "I remember days when humans came to the mountain seeking wisdom, listening to the wind, water, and earth. They honoured the ancient animals and respected the land. But now, they come seeking conquest, seeking to claim the mountains' power for themselves." The creature's eyes locked onto Timmy's, filled with urgency. "The disconnection is deep, but it's not too late. Humans can remember. They can still listen to the whispers of the wind and respect the balance if they wish to."

His voice rose, emphasizing the importance of Timmy's role in this story. "You, Timmy, as one of the humans, are part of this story. Your actions, your choices, can shift the balance. Will you promise me to remember the old ways? The natural bond humans shared with us wildlings?"

The weight of the words settled upon Timmy like a call to action to reclaim humanity's connection to their ancient friend, Nature. He nodded. "Yes, I promise you. I will never forget the deep bond I share with the natural world."

"The time has come for humanity to remember," the Yeti continued, pleased at Timmy's response. "The time is here for them to respect the natural world, to honour the balance."

He finished speaking, and the cave fell silent, with only the crackling flames of the fire. Timmy looked at Lythari and saw him all curled up by the fire, fast asleep. He must have heard these tales so many times, Timmy thought, and gave out a soft laugh. Lythari's small round eyes opened slowly, and the two friends looked at each other for a long time. Timmy gave him a kind smile, and Lythari smiled back. It was apparently too simple a moment, but between the two of them, it was of immense significance.

Finally, Lythari stood up. "Our time here is limited, Timmy. We must go now." Timmy nodded.

When they were leaving, the Yeti handed Timmy a small crystal.

"A token of our friendship" he said.

The crystal glowed with an ethereal light, its translucent surface reflecting hues of sapphire and amethyst and shimmering like the night sky.

Intricate patterns etched into its facets seemed to hold ancient wisdom. Shaped like a snowflake, delicate and symmetrical, it fit comfortably in the palm of Timmy's hand, radiating warmth and energy. When he held it up to the light of the fire, the crystal cast a rainbow-colored aura. Its presence seemed to calm Timmy's mind and soothe his heart.

"I have imbued the crystal with the essence of the Himalayas, and infused it with the mountains' ancient power and wisdom. It will serve as a reminder of your connection to the natural world and your responsibility towards it" the Yeti clarified.

Timmy thanked him, and promised to protect the mountains' majesty. With a final wave at the gigantic enigma, Timmy descended the mountain with Lythari guiding the way, the crystal secure in his pocket.

As they stepped back through the portal onto his terrace, Timmy turned to Lythari. "That was incredible!"

Lythari smiled. "You should have gotten used to this by now, young friend" he teased. "Now, if you'll excuse me, I'll take your leave." He bowed, continuing to pull Timmy's leg.

Timmy laughed. "Already?" he said, then looking around and realising it was almost morning, added, "I'll see you again soon?"

The Guardian nodded. "Soon" he assured, and spread out his wings into the sky.

Back in his bed, Timmy clutched the crystal from the Yeti close to his heart. His mind replayed the wondrous adventure he had just had. He couldn't believe he had seen a Yeti outside his story books, and not only seen, but also talked to!

The Yeti's words echoed in his mind again and again. *Respect the natural world, and it will respect you.*

Timmy's mind raced.Should he tell his parents about Lythari and the incredible adventures?Or should he keep them hidden, and keep sharing them as dreams, like he has been doing for the past three plus years, protecting his secret world?But Lythari himself had asked him to not lie for his sake. And Timmy had a feeling if he didn't confess everything now, this would turn into a habit for him. But his fear of disbelief and scepticism wrestled with his longing for honesty. He weighed the possible consequences.

If he shared, would his parents think he had lost his grip on reality? Would they dismiss his experiences as mere fantasy?

But if he kept quiet, the guilt of deception would consume him.

He remembered how Lythari had asked him to use his creativity positively and to always be truthful to the ones who deserved it. He started thinking again. His parents were definitely the two people who deserved the most to know his stories. They had only ever wanted what was the best for their son.

Timmy stared at the crystal. In the darkness of the room, it looked like just another ordinary stone. Timmy rubbed it absent-mindedly.

Suddenly, a gentle breeze rustled the curtains, and Timmy heard a rough whispering voice that said, "Courage is not the complete absence of fear, but the will to act despite."

Timmy nodded determinedly. His resolve solidified. He would take the leap of faith. He drifted off to a morning slumber only to be woken less than an hour later by the alarm's loud ringing.

After brushing his teeth and changing into his daytime clothes, He walked out of his room, ready to share his secret with his parents.

For a moment, he stopped, he considered hiding the crystal, but something inside him shifted.

He couldn't bear the thought of deceiving his parents again. Taking a deep breath, Timmy put the crystal in his pocket, and approached his parents' bedroom.

It was a Saturday and it was ritual that his parents slept in late, while he prepared the cereal and called grandma to give the weekly updates. But today, he couldn't wait for that long. He felt sorry because the previous day was a long day at the Fest and he knew his parents must be tired, but he couldn't contain the excitement in his tiny heart.

FIFTEEN

THE REVEAL

"Mummy, Daddy" Timmy called, standing in his parents' bedroom where they were fast asleep.

Hearing their son's voice out of nowhere, Mr and Mrs Tint woke up hurriedly. "What's wrong, what's wrong?" Mr Tint inquired, while his wife scrambled for her glasses on the bedside table.

"I– um– I need to tell you something" Timmy said, his voice trembling slightly. He sat down on the bed.

"Well go on, sweetie. What is it?" Mrs Tint encouraged, wearing her glasses. Yawning widely and sounding very groggy.

Suddenly, Timmy went utterly speechless. He couldn't think of a single thing to say, or rather, he didn't know where to start. Not knowing what to do, he pulled out the crystal from his pocket and held it up for his parents to see. Mr and Mrs Tint exchanged confused glances.

"I've been having these... adventures" he said, then noticing that made them even more confused, added, "With Lythari." As soon as he took the name, he felt a jolt of confidence rush through his body.

Mrs Tint put her hand on her son's shoulder. "Okay, honey, your dream buddy. We believe you. You want to talk about it?" in an attempt to sound empathetic, but Timmy did not miss that she exchanged glances with her husband that clearly said she did not.

Timmy nodded. He took a deep breath, and then began recounting his journeys with Lythari – their adventures with Puck, visiting Merland, the shell-pendant, meeting the Yeti, learning about the natural world, and receiving the crystal.

His parents listened attentively, and they gasped here and there in awe and disbelief. When Timmy finished, the room fell silent.

Mrs Tint was the first one to speak up. "Well, that's a lot to take in, Timmy. For over three years you've been telling us these were your dreams, now you say it's real?" She couldn't hold up her empathetic, all understanding stance anymore.

Timmy nodded understandingly. He had prepared himself for this.

"But" she continued, "What I do want you to know is that your Daddy and I are proud of you for being honest and brave." Then looking at her husband, who still staring at the crystal that Timmy was held in disbelief, nudged him. "Aren't we?" she looked very weak, trying hard to mask her vulnerability.

Mr Tint started. "What. Oh yes, right. Yes, son, we are proud of you. We'll support you no matter what" he stammered, and then forced a worried but understanding smile.

Timmy smiled back. He felt a weight lift off his shoulders. For the first time, he felt truly understood. Well, maybe not yet, but this was the beginning. At least his parents tried. They were being utterly supportive.

The crystal, once a secret, now symbolized his newfound openness and connection with his parents. Lythari had been right. Honesty was indeed the best, he thought, as he hugged his parents tightly, and then left the room with a heart full of relief.

However, as soon as he stepped out of his parents' room and shut their door, Timmy heard the sound of sobs from inside. His mother was crying. He hesitated, wondering if he should just leave. But something told him that this was about him, and what he had just told them. He put his ear close to the door, and listened.

It seemed to him his parents were having a very serious conversation about something.

"...six years ago," Timmy heard his father say.

"I remember I was pregnant with our second child," his mother answered. "And I had severe preeclampsia. The doctors said bed rest was the only option."

"Yes, yes I remember those days vividly, inside my mind. Though we had promised never to bring up the topic ever again, to let it rest in the past...here we are..." his father's voice seemed to crack.

Timmy's ears perked up. He remembered how when he was four years old, he was sent to his grandparents' house for five whole months because his mother was very ill. But he never knew that she was pregnant, that he was to have a sibling. He pressed his ears.

"Poor kid, he was only four," his father was saying. "And we had to send him to my mothers' for a few months. You were not allowed out of bed and I had to keep earning, we couldn't afford a day-care and who else could have handled our dear little Timmy who at that age loved to jump and run and climb all the time"

"Then we got the puppy to keep him company, because he was an active toddler and mom's hands were too full to keep him interested continuously" said his mother.

"I thought once the baby was born and everything was back to normal, as we bring him and the pup back together. But...but I lost the baby...the doctors tried everything but couldn't save her.. " her voice broke as she supressed tears.

" I never thought we would be discussing this aloud ever again, but only God knows how many times these thoughts crossed my mind in the past 6 years. Because the pup was named Lythari and the friend in Timmy's dreams is also Lythari, I had an intuition several times that there must be a link" she continued, in between sniffs and sobs.

Timmy's eyes widened. He couldn't believe what he was hearing. A brother or sister he never knew? A pup? A pup named Lythari? Why doesn't he remember any of this?

"Those were some nightmarish days, I won't lie. The grief consumed us totally, and then you descended into depression. Lord knows how terribly helpless I felt at that time, to handle the loss and not allow Timmy to feel anything about it...while continuing at work" his father said, weeping softly.

"I know, dear. But what else could we have done? Those were tough times, and I couldn't bear the thought of raising the innocent little puppy, he was a constant reminder of my loss, I had planned to raise the three of them together, but...but I thought he was unlucky" his mother said in a voice full of guilt. "Or so, the depression made me think".

"It wasn't your fault, honey. Even I supported the decision to not bring the puppy back home. With taking care of the household, making sure of your recovery and ensuring none of these affected Timmy's vital developmental years, I too couldn't have practically put in the effort at that point," his father tried to reassure her. Even though he didn't sound convincing to himself.

"So we decided to rehome him to a loving family who were properly equipped to give him the care he needed. That beautiful little snowy Husky. .now that I'm thinking these thoughts aloud, I do too feel a pinch of guilt in having to let him go..."

"Husky?!" Timmy thought startled. "That's MY Lythari they're talking about"

Timmy opened the door a little bit. His parents were sitting on their bed; his father was holding his mother in his arms as she sobbed into his chest, while tears streamed down his face as well.

"Sometimes, when Timmy told us those stories of adventure in his dreams, I'd wonder why his friend had to be called Lythari," his mother said, her voice muffled in her father's shirt. "We just never asked." she asked, looking up at her husband.

"I still wonder what happened to the husky pup. I was too sick to take him to his new home myself, and you literally had no time to, did Mum tell you anything about him in the last six years? Never mentioned? We talk to her every weekend and spend every summer at her place, but never asked again out of guilt"

His father shook her head. "I have no idea about that. I remember when I had reached Mother's house to bring Timmy back, after you were home from the hospital, she was the one who told me about the family that were eager to adopt the puppy and that she will take care of it. I was too stressed to look into it more deeply, I let her handle the matter," he said. "But I never really asked her again about Lythari. His topic always filled me with grief at being unable to give him a home and separating him from Timmy. I'm sure though Mum ensured he was rehomed properly, given how much she loved and cared for him."

"Looking back, now that we all are healed, I strongly feel Getting rid of Lythari was a big mistake. He could have helped my scarred mind and heart recover faster and Timmy would have had him in reality," his mother admitted.

His father nodded, agreeing with her.

"It was like losing a part of us. A part of Timmy," his mother realised. "His unconscious mind retained the memory of the name Lythari, and that explains the dreams , I suppose. but what Timmy's dream buddy Lythari looks likes, I wonder. But, beyond dreams? Him percieving all these as reality? He must be having some subconscious scars..."

"Yes. what worries me is, our boy is confused between dreams and reality. How could all that he just told us be real?" his father whispered.

" We need to know more , in details, from him, before we think of taking him to the school counselor. he must know that we do believe him." his mother agreed.

" Maybe that will help us all get the closure" Mr Tint sighed.

"For all of us." Mrs Tint chimed in weakly.

His mother's tears subsided. The room fell silent, and the air filled with regret and longing. Longing for Lythari, the loyal companion. For the memories the two of them could have shared. For the love they'd lost. And found it again. Through Timmy's dreams. And, for life must go on. One cannot dwell on losses forever.

Lythari's return had sparked hope in them.

Hope for reunion

For redemption.

For healing.

At that moment, the past and present intertwined, as they sat there wondering what the future held for Lythari and Timmy's relationship. And for them too.

Timmy's heart ached. He closed the door as gently as he could, then started walking towards his own room. His parents' conversation gradually drifted off into tears and silence.

Timmy's mind Reeled. He knew the pup they were talking about and His Lythari were the same. Lythari's return in his dream wasn't just coincidental. It was a connection. A connection meant to be. A connection with his family's past. To the pain and grief they had ensured, the love and hope they had lost and regained again. Timmy's heart swelled with understanding.

He suddenly felt he had grown up beyond his years in those few minutes. He realised his parent's scars ran deeper than they ever let him see. His heart filled with gratitude as he realised, so did their love, their love for him. And for each other.

Now Timmy understood why Lythari always keeps talking about their bond and connection. Because it wasn't a normal one. The Guardian had a connection to his family's past, to the pain and grief they'd endured.

Timmy's heart swelled as it all started to make sense gradually. He felt bad for all those times he had given his parents a hard time, not listening to them, lying to them.

Timmy had reached his room. Entering, he shut the door, and took out the crystal from his pocket, now glowing with some newfound significance. Timmy wondered what it could be, and almost immediately realised.

Lythari's story was far from over.

He was ready to listen. Lythari had always been there for him, through thick and thin. This was the time he needed to be there for the Angel. If he wanted to talk about himself and his past, Timmy would just listen, instead of dismissing it and brushing it under the carpet.

The crystal glowed again, and Timmy closed his eyes and wished for Lythari to be there with him at the time. That would be a miracle, he thought. But honestly, he was too used to seeing miracles now, and nothing seemed impossible.

SIXTEEN

SAVING AN UNICORN

A few days passed. One night Timmy was just about to drift off to sleep.

There was the sound of a thin "pop", and as soon as Timmy opened his eyes, they sparkled with excitement as Lythari materialized before him, his eyes warm and kind as always.

"Lythari, thank you so much for coming! I was just thinking about you" Timmy leapt.

Lythari smiled. "I know," he replied. "Tell me, dear friend, what is it that you need?"

"I was wondering if– if you could tell me a bit about yourself, Lythari" Timmy said pleadingly.

Lythari's expression turned evasive. "Another time, young one," he said. "Besides, you already know everything about me." He chuckled.

But Timmy pressed on.

"No, not that. I want to know about your past. Where did you come from?" he urged, curious.

Lythari's gaze darted around the room. "I don't think this is a conversation we should be having right now, Timmy. Your dreams are more important. I'll tell you everything once you're the right age an–"

"I'm grown enough!" Timmy interrupted him, his curiosity growing. "Please, Lythari, I want to know. What happened to you after you left our house?"

Lythari's face clouded. " your house? What?"

He deftly diverted the topic: "An urgent matter requires our attention" he said abruptly, his eyes genuinely alarmed.

Timmy looked deep into the eyes of his friend. He realised that Lythari had, in reality, never lied to him or misled him. So, when he of all people was refusing to answer his questions, there must be some valid reason behind it. He decided not to push the matter any farther.

"What is it, Lythari?" he asked, dropping the subject and deciding to help his loyal companion.

Lythari gave him a slight nod, as if he understood what just happened. "In the Enchanted Forest, young friend. A unicorn needs our help."

"A unicorn?" Timmy repeated.

"Yes. She's been trapped by the Dark forces" Lythari explained.

Timmy was genuinely concerned. "We must rescue her at once! I'm ready, Lythari, let's go" he said determinedly.

Lythari nodded. "So we will, my friend, so we will."

Saying this, Lythari spread his wings as always and Timmy climbed onto his back. With a swift gesture, the Guardian transported them to the Enchanted Forest.

As they ventured into the forest, magic and danger lurked around every corner.

Lythari's own story would have to wait, Timmy thought. The unicorn's fate took precedence, and they must save her from the evil. But deep down somewhere, his resolve remained unwavering. He would save the unicorn, as well as uncover Lythari's secrets. He knew what he had to do.

The two of them ventured deeper, and the moonlight filtering through the canopy above cast eerie shadows on the ground. The air vibrated with an otherworldly, supernatural energy.

Eventually, their quest led them to a clearing, where Timmy spotted a magnificent unicorn lay wounded. Her coat, once shimmering silver as Lythari informed him, was now dulled by dirt and blood. Her horn, once radiant, now cracked and dim.

Timmy's heart swelled with compassion for the helpless creature before his eyes. He looked at his friend. "Lythari, we must do something about this. Please tell me how we can help her" he pleaded, his eyes welling up.

Lythari approached the unicorn, his eyes scanning her injuries. "Dark magic binds her" he whispered. "We must break the curse. And for that, we must not break down, Timmy, but work together to save the poor creature."

Timmy rubbed his eyes with the back of his hands, nodding determinedly. "You're right. We should get to work right away. Tell me what to do, Lythari."

"Take out your crystal, Timmy. The one the Yeti gave you" Lythari instructed, and at the same time waved his wings twice in the air. A long, beautiful flute appeared. The Angel grabbed it by his wings, and starting playing a soothing melody on his flute.

As he was channelling the crystal's energy by rubbing it with his fingers, Timmy listened to the calm, peaceful melody that his friend played, and it seemed to him that he had been transported to a whole new world altogether, a world where everything was tranquil and magical, a world devoid of hate and full of only love and joy.

Suddenly, Lythari stopped playing, and Timmy was pulled out of his trance. He looked before him, and saw that the unicorn's eyelids were flickering. Within a few seconds, its eyes opened slowly.

"The music of this flute has merged with the crystal's energy, and the dark magic has begun to dissipate" Lythari explained with a satisfactory sigh.

Timmy's face broke into a smile as he saw the unicorn's horn glowing again. With newfound strength, the magnificent creature stood up. Her white coat shimmered in the light coming out from the crystal. Her mane flowed like silk. Timmy and Lythari looked at each other, smiling, and were about to bid her goodbye when the bushes behind them rustled. The three of them turned around, and realised that their triumph had indeed been short-lived.

For there emerged from the shadows the Dark Sorcerer, the one whom Lythari had told Timmy about on their way to the forest.

Timmy was horror-stricken as the dangerous wizard walked up to them. He wore a green robe that covered most of his body, but his black, burnt, crinkled face was visible clearly, where his bloodshot eyes blazed with malice.

"Ah Lythari, we meet again. And who is this kid with you? You shouldn't have meddled in the Dark Sorcerer's business. Get ready to pay" he snarled, showing large, pointed teeth where maggots grew and saliva dripped from.

Lythari stood tall. Timmy grasped the crystal.

The Sorcerer took out his wand from under his robe and waved it in the air. A bolt of dark energy was unleashed.

But the two friends were fast. Lythari jumped high in the air and deflected the force of Evil with his flute, while Timmy, once again, channelled the crystal's power. A shield of purple light formed around them, and it's force was so strong that the Sorcerer's wand was thrown off.

The unicorn, now healed, joined the battle. Her horn shone brighter, making the Sorcerer stumble back.

He fell on his knees to the ground, and his body slowly boiled, distorted, bubbled and melted away grostequely, hence defeated.

Suddenly, Timmy saw fireflies emerging from the darkness around, and they started dancing. The trees began to sing and wave in joy. It was as if the entire forest had erupted in celebration.

Lythari smiled, as he waved his wings once more and the flute vanished. Timmy placed the crystal carefully inside his pocket.

The unicorn muzzled him. "Only the pure-hearted could have defeated the Dark Sorcerer, Timmy, one who is devoid of all evil and cruelty. Your heart is in the right place" he whispered. "You and Lythari are true heroes."

As they bid farewell to the unicorn and to the Enchanted Forest, Lythari turned to Timmy.

"Your bravery is remarkable," he said. "But by now, honestly, I expect nothing less from you."

Timmy beamed.

After a while, Lythari's expression turned serious. "But our journey is far from over," he said solemnly. "The Dark forces are not completely destroyed. And they gather. More adventures await us, Timmy."

Timmy stood firm. "Whatever comes our way, we'll sail through it together" he promised.

The two of them looked at each other, and Timmy hugged his friend even tighter. They vanished into the night sky, ready to face whatever lay ahead. Together.

SEVENTEEN

THE LOST CITY OF GOLD

It was a Monday morning. Sunlight streamed through the kitchen window, casting a warm glow.

The Tints sat together at the breakfast table. Mr and Mrs Tint were having sandwiches and fruit juice. Timmy munched on his cereal, lost in thought.

"So, Timmy," Mrs Tint began, a soft smile etched on her face, longing palpable. "Tell us more about Lythari."

"Yes. Did you go on an adventure last night?" Mr Tint asked, his eyes curious with childlike wonder.

Timmy's spoon froze mid-air. In the thrill of last night's journey, he had forgotten all about asking Lythari about his past after they were done with the adventure.

"Um, he's– he's amazing. All's good, Mummy," he mumbled, then before his father could repeat his question, he quickly added, "I'm running late for school, Daddy. I'll draw a picture of him to show you how he looks, when I get back in the evening." He didn't want them to suspect his eavesdropping.

His parents nodded, intrigued, trying hard not to make their eagerness too obvious.

"Okay! I can't wait to see it," Mr Tint exclaimed. "And hear more about your adventures!"

Timmy grinned. "Tonight" he promised.

He gulped down the remaining cereal in one go, grabbed his backpack from the table, and rushed out of the door.

The whole day at school passed in a blur. Timmy's mind wandered, replaying Lythari's stories and wondering what he would tell his parents once he got back. Then, he remembered his resolution. No more lies, he thought. Just then, the final bell rang, and Timmy, along with the other students, boarded the school bus.

Once the bus dropped him off at the stop, Timmy hurried home, eagerness building inside him. Bursting through the door, he dropped his backpack on the floor and greeted his parents, both of whom were sitting on the couch, sipping tea.

"Hi, Mummy! Hi, Daddy!" Before they could respond, he added, "Time to create!"

His parents laughed out loud. "Dear, do get yourself freshened up first. We are in no hurry" said his mother in an amused voice.

"But *I* am! I can't wait to show Lythari to you" Timmy replied, his voice restless, as he took out the paper, pencils, colours from his school bag and placed them on the kitchen table.

Not wanting to curb their child's enthusiasm, Mr and Mrs Tint gathered round, their eyes round with eagerness and excitement.

Timmy bent down at the table, and began his drawing. His parents' eyes widened as Lythari's image began to take shape. Timmy's pencil scratched across the paper to give the finishing touches, and there he was, Lythari, the friend he couldn't stop talking about, as if brought to life on paper.

His drawing depicted a majestic dog with snow-white fur, large, iridescent wings sprouting from his back, a pair of round brown-red eyes shining bright like amber, and a grey muzzle. The wings seemed crafted from shimmering dove feathers, and the fur near his ears was rendered in soft, flowing lines, with shades of golden brown, grey and cream. A gentle smile curved his lips.

Timmy had also added intricate details. Lythari's collar was adorned with tiny, glittering stars, and there was a delicate, sparkling necklace around his neck, bearing a miniature crystal. The flute, slung over Lythari's shoulder, was etched with whimsical patterns. Wings spread wide on two sides, Lythari seemed to soar off the page and into the room.

Mr and Mrs Tint marvelled at the drawing. There was no doubt in their minds, anymore, regarding Lythari's identity. They exchanged a meaningful glance, understanding, longing, a tiny little speck of guilt and hope all played at the same time.

"He looks magnificent, Timmy! His wings are stunning, did you not draw him in the painting at your art competition during the school fest? why did'nt you tell us then? though that was'nt this detailed…" said Mrs Tint. "Also, honey, is that the crystal you showed us the other day? The one around his neck?" she asked.

"The one from the– what had you said, Yeti, if I'm not wrong?" Mr Tint chimed in.

Timmy laughed. "Yes. The one from the Yeti. I added that detail by myself. Just thought, he'd look good with it. He actually doesn't always wear it though, just in my drawing"

"He does look really handsome" his parents agreed. Hiding the curiosity in their voice.

Timmy beamed with pride. "Well, that's Lythari. My one true friend and my guide in every difficult situation."

His parents, too, exchanged a look of pride. They knew their son's imagination was boundless. But this time it wasn't just that. They were familiar with the creature that lay etched on Timmy's page. Perhaps, just perhaps, there was more to Lythari's story than they knew.

They sat beside their son as he packed his stuff up from the table, and patted him on the shoulders.

After a few more silent but meaningful glances, Mr Tint spoke: "where does he come from?"

Timmy shrugged his shoulders, "I've never thought of asking"

"We'd love to meet Lythari, you say he is real, not just your dream buddy, can we meet him?" said Mrs Tint, curiosity shining in her eyes.

"Can you arrange that?" asked Mr Tint, sharing his wife's eagerness.

Timmy hesitated. He couldn't promise them anything without asking Lythari first.

"I'll ask him next time he visits. But I can't promise" he answered.

His parents nodded. "We understand" they said. "But just let your special friend know we are eager to meet him."

Timmy smiled. "I will. Thanks, Mummy, Daddy."

That night, after having dinner and then completing his homework, Timmy didn't go to bed instantly. He still had an important job to do. He owed someone else the truth as well.

He asked his mother if he could borrow her phone. She agreed, and Timmy went up to his room and dialled Emma's number. After two rings, she picked up. "Timmy?" came her voice.

"Hey, Emma!" he said, excitement building.

"Hey! What's up?" she replied.

"All good. Listen, I need to tell you something" Timmy said urgently.

"Can't wait till school? I'm sleepy," Emma teased, faking a dramatic yawning. "Is everything okay though?" she added in a concerning tone.

"Yeah, it's just...I have a confession to make. To you" Timmy said.

"To me? Well, go ahead, then" Emma urged in her chirpy sing song manner.

"No. You're right. Not over phone. It's pretty late now, sorry I didn't notice" Timmy said apologetically.

"Tomorrow, at recess?" Emma suggested.

"Deal!" Timmy agreed, and hung up the call.

The secret would soon be shared, he thought. After his parents, he wanted Emma to be the first person to know about the truth of Lythari and their magical adventures together. Beyond just dream stories that almost the whole school knows, as him 'fabricating tales'. Timmy's heart swelled with anticipation. For the first time in months, he couldn't wait for school the next day.

That night, Lythari visited Timmy with a serious expression on his face.

At first, Timmy couldn't make out what he was so worried about, so he tried to change the subject. "Lythari, tell me more about yourself" he insisted. "You know, before you became... magical. What was your life on earth like?"

Lythari looked at him evasively. "Who said I had a life on earth?" he asked, then, before he could respond and to Timmy's relief, added, "Besides, we have more pressing matters tonight."

"But I want to know" Timmy pleaded. "Where did you come from?"

Lythari's gaze drifted. "Far-off lands" he murmured, making this eyes roll dramatically, and leaning in for effect.

"Could you be more specific?" Timmy pressed, serious.

Lythari gave a tiny but weak smile. "Your determination is admirable, I must say."

"You only have yourself to blame, my friend" Timmy teased, and the two of them shared a laugh.

"Very well. I'll tell you. But not today. Another time, perhaps, but I surely will. Now, we've got a pressing matter that requires our attention" Lythari entreated.

Understanding the graveness of the situation and satisfied with Lythari's promise, Timmy asked, "Tell me, Lythari, what is it?"

"The Lost City of Gold" announced the Guardian. "There's an ancient artefact hidden within, that holds the key to balancing the cosmos. Only you, Timmy, can retrieve it" he informed.

Timmy's eyes widened.

"Me?"

Lythari nodded. "You are the Chosen One" he declared.

Timmy felt chills run down his spine. For a moment, he thought he was soaring. But then he looked at Lythari, who gave him a warm smile. "I am with you, Timmy, don't worry. You won't be alone in this journey" he said reassuringly.

The Lost City of Gold beckoned him. Timmy realised the massive responsibility he had on his shoulders, and vowed to prove himself deserving of it. He stood before Lythari with determination etched on his face, and said, "I'm prepared. Let's embark."

Lythari smiled and nodded. With a wave of his wings, the room dissolved into a swirling vortex.

Timmy felt the rush of wind, his stomach lurching.

When the vortex cleared, he found himself standing amidst a lush jungle. Exotic birds sang, and vines and creepers snaked around ancient stone structures.

"The Lost City of Gold" Lythari whispered , paralysed in wonder and amazement.

Hidden deep within the jungle, the city shimmered like a mirage. Ancient structures, cloaked in trailing plants and spider webs, stretched toward the sky. The air vibrated with secrets and mysteries.

As Timmy and Lythari ventured deeper, the city revealed its treasures to them. Golden spires that refracted sunlight into kaleidoscopic colours, intricate mosaics depicting ancient battles and mythological creatures, halls lined with glittering jewels and precious artefacts, and the Central Plaza, where a majestic fountain sang a melodic tune. Waterfalls cascaded down crystal rocks, filling the air with misty veils.

The architecture of the city blended seamlessly into the jungle, where trees grew through the temple's crumbling walls and flowers bloomed in every colour. Exotic birds flitted from statue to statue, and the scent of sandalwood and myrrh wafted through the air. In the distance, the sounds of the jungle pulsed. Timmy could hear monkeys chattering, parrots squawking, and drums beating in the heart of the forest. They walked far and long, the setting sun hung below the horizon, twilight progressed as the chirp of crickets grew louder.

As night descended and darkness engulfed the surroundings, the city transformed. Stars twinkled like diamonds, torches flickered on the temple gate, casting shadows, and the radiance of the Golden Orb illuminated the temple. With night, Timmy felt the city turned from a deserted mysterious realm to one of wonder, a dream world of fantasy, where myth and magic intertwined.

"Hidden deep within the city, the artefact awaits." Lythari reminded him.

They had arrived at the Temple of the Golden Orb, which stood at the heart of the city, towering above the ruins. Its entrance, flanked by large twin stone statues, seemed to whisper tales of forgotten civilizations. The eyes of the statues, piercing into Timmy's eyes and unyielding, guarded the secrets of the temple. The daunting structures looked at him as if daring him to enter the temple. Timmy hesitated.

"Courage, Timmy. I'm here with you." Lythari's reassuring voice came from behind, and Timmy shook his fear away.

They approached the temple, and suddenly, a strange thing happened. The statues at the temple gate sprang to life, their stone wings spread wide. Timmy and Lythari prepared for an attack, but it never came. Instead, the statues kept staring at them, as if trying to burn them into ash just by their gaze.

Timmy and Lythari dodged the deadly gaze of the life-like statues, and entered through the huge crumbling gate, and once inside the temple, darkness enveloped them.

Lythari's flute illuminated the path. Timmy took out his crystal and rubbed it, and it shone with a red light, which he then held up as a torch along the path.

Through treacherous tunnels and chambers, they ventured, navigating deadly traps and avoiding poison darts. They crossed a chasm on a precarious bridge, and finally reached the heart of the temple.

There, embedded within the envelope of darkness, lay a glittering chamber filled with gold. At its centre, an artefact shone – the Golden Orb – radiating strong, mystic energy.

But as Timmy stepped forward to grab the Golden Orb, a solemn figure emerged from within the darkness. Timmy rubbed the crystal once more, and it shone brighter, revealing the figure's face to Timmy. Standing before him was a treasure hunter, with a bow in his one hand, and a knife in the other, arrows on his back, and a malicious grin etched on his fiendish face. Timmy understood that the man had come there to steal the Golden Orb for his own profit, which he couldn't let happen.

"Mine" the hunter snarled.

Timmy stood tall.

"Not under my watch" he replied.

He turned around and looked at Lythari, who pointed his wing at the crystal in Timmy's hand. Timmy grinned, turned back at the rival, and harnessed the crystal's power.

A blast of energy shot out from the crystal. It repelled the hunter, as its force pushed him down onto the ground, and summoned the orb with a bright, red ray of light. The orb floated towards Timmy, and he grasped it, feeling its warmth.

As soon as Timmy clutched the Golden Orb, the city began to tremble. Cracks appeared on the walls of the temple and the chasm started rumbling and overflowing.

"Time to leave" Lythari announced, and snatched Timmy's hand with one of his wings. With one final glance at the crumbling city, Timmy leaped onto the Guardian's back, and flew out of the temple as it collapsed into pieces.

They escaped into the night sky, and the Lost City of Gold vanished into the jungle.

As Lythari deposited Timmy safely into his room, Timmy's heart beat faster than ever.

Lythari smiled. "Well done, Timmy" he said, a proud look on his face.

The power of the Golden Orb coursed through Timmy. He sensed a newfound confidence blooming inside him. "What to do with this now, Lythari?" he asked, pointing at the shining object.

"Keep it safe with you. We'll need it in the future" Lythari stated.

Timmy placed the orb delicately in the innermost drawer of his closet. He then locked the drawer, kept the key in one of his pyjamas' pockets that he never wore, and settled into bed, his mind racing with everything that had happened that day.

Lythari laid beside him, a gentle smile on his face.

After a while Timmy decided to nudge him again. He knew what Lythari's response would be, but he wanted to hear it from him.

"Lythari, I need to know," Timmy said in a calm voice. "Your origins, your past, all of it. It's really important that you tell me."

Lythari's expression introspective. After a long pause, he said, "Very well, Timmy. But promise me you'll try to understand."

"Of course I will, Lythari" Timmy vowed.

"Alright then. Next dream, I'll take you on that journey. The journey to my past. But tell me one thing," he continued, "Why do you suddenly want to know about it?"

Timmy considered for a while. He felt it was too soon to tell Lythari about the conversation between his parents about his past that he had overheard. As long as Lythari himself doesn't tell him anything, he shouldn't know Timmy knows things about him. That would be too hurtful, he thought.

"My parents know about you. I told them. And they were very excited. They want to meet you" he said finally.

Lythari's eyes widened. "Are you certain? *They* want to meet *Me*" he asked sounding genuinely confused.

Timmy knew why, but he didn't want to be explicit, he nodded simply in response trying to keep his face from displaying any emotions.

"They've been asking questions. The pendant, the crystal, they're questioning and I couldn't continue lying".

Lythari's face softened. "I'd love to meet them. I'll arrange a meeting soon," he promised. "But promise me they won't get scared or treat me indecently on seeing me?" he asked.

"I promise. I know they won't , still, I will make sure they don't" Timmy assured him.

"Fine then. In your next dream, we'll embark on two journeys. One to uncover my past, and the other to meet your parents."

Timmy's face glowed with excitement.

"Thank you, Lythari."

Lythari's smile mirrored Timmy's.

"Sleep tight, young adventurer."

The Angel vanished, and Timmy drifted into deep slumber.

His heart was filled with anticipation for his next dream.

For the secrets to be unveiled.

For Lythari's story to unfold.

EIGHTEEN

EMMA NOW KNOWS

The morning sunlight streamed through the classroom windows, casting a warm glow on Timmy's eager face. He couldn't wait for lunch break, when he could finally share his incredible secrets with Emma.

Throughout the morning classes, Timmy's mind seemed to wander off far away. Math problems blurred together, and History lessons faded into the background, while his thoughts drifted to Lythari and the Lost City of Gold.

Finally, the lunch bell rang. Timmy grabbed his backpack and rushed to meet Emma.

They settled into their favourite corner of the schoolyard, under the shade of a tall oak tree, surrounded by vibrant flowers.

Emma unwrapped her sandwich. "Spill, Timmy" she said eagerly. "What's been going on?" bobbing her head. Classic Emma Style.

Timmy took a deep breath.

"Lythari," he said. "Lythari has been going on."

"Ah, the magical creature," Emma's eyes sparkled. "I knew it! Tell me everything." She said specifically emphasising on the 'kn' of knew and banging her little fists on her lunch box.

Timmy smiled. "I don't know where to begin. So, I'll just start from last night." Emma nodded, and Timmy began his tale.

The Temple of the Golden Orb.

The Lost City of Gold.

The hunter.

The unicorn.

The Dark Sorcerer.

The Yeti.

Merland.

The shell pendant and the crystal.

Emma listened, awestruck. She had completely forgotten about her sandwich, and now listened to Timmy with her eyes and jaw wide opened. Occasionally, Timmy would get a "Whoa!" from her in response. He wondered in between the storytelling if she forgot to blink or breathe. She was so immersed, so invested. How could he keep this away from her for so long, his only best friend since toddlerhood, the most genuinely helpful, innocent and well-meaning girl in the entire school who could turn into a fighter if it's for Timmy.

"Then there's more," Timmy continued. "My parents know about Lythari. They want to meet him."

Emma's jaw dropped further, she tilted her head to the side to almost touch the grass, if that was even possible. "Please go on. I literally have zero idea what to say right now, Face palm!" was all she could manage.

Timmy laughed.

"Lythari promised to arrange a meeting with them. My parents, I mean," he said, then looking at Emma's gobsmacked expression, added, "Yeah, I know. It's unbelievable to me too. Especially now that I'm saying it out loud."

"So, wait," Emma stopped him. "That whole story about Alex and Dave, it was you all along? The flying boy? Why did you lie to me, Timmy?" she said, hurt.

Timmy nodded. "Yes. Yes, I'm sorry, Emma. I shouldn't have lied to you. That is the confession I was talking about on the phone. You deserved better than that," he said, then added, "Yes, it was me. I am the flying boy." Then he told her about the conversation about Lythari's past that he had overheard between his parents.

Emma listened with rapt attention. Once Timmy was done, her expression turned thoughtful. "That's quite a tale. But Timmy, be careful," she said in a concerned voice. "This is all so very...magical. And knowing you, I know you love it. But remember that it's also very unknown."

Timmy knew he had nothing to fear about Lythari, but he also knew that Emma's concern was coming from a place of love and care.

"Don't worry, Emma. I trust Lythari. I will trust him with my life" he said softly, assuring her.

Emma smiled. "That's great then. If you love him so much, he must be really great. I'm with you, Timmy. Always." She chuckled, chirpy Emma was back. She believed him wholeheartedly.

Timmy smiled back. "Um, is there anything else that you want to know?"

Emma thought for a second. "No. I don't think so," she said, "Unless – "

"Go on," Timmy urged.

"Timmy, I want to be there too. When Lythari tells his story, and when he meets your parents." She looked like she will break into one of her 'please please' dances right now.

Timmy hesitated. "I don't know, Emma. It's all very...personal, you know."

Emma's face fell. "But Dude! I'm your best friend," she pleaded, trying to fake offense. "I want to support you."

Timmy's resolve wavered. "Well, I try, but Lythari might not agree" he said with a grounding exhale.

Emma's persistence didn't falter.

"Please, Timmy. I'll be quiet, I promise." She had now broken into her seated dance which Timmy was apprehending.

Timmy sighed. "Okay, fine" he said. "But you have to promise me one thing."

"Anything" Emma replied with abroad broad smile.

"You have to trust Lythari. And not ask too many questions."

Emma nodded eagerly. "I promise."

Timmy's expression turned serious. "You know, Emma," he said, looking up at her, "There's something I've noticed," he said. "Lythari diverts the subject whenever I ask about his past. He doesn't want to talk about it for some reason."

Emma's brow furrowed. "That's weird" she responded.

"Yeah. I think he's hiding something. Some really deep secrets, which he doesn't to share even with me."

Emma placed her hand on Timmy's.

"From what I just heard of Lythari from you, I'm sure that if he is, after all, hiding something from you, he has his reasons for it. Either it's something extremely personal to him, or he thinks that the secrets are going to hurt you, and are better not revealed. But don't worry, Timmy. We'll uncover the truth together."

At that moment, the school bell rang, signalling the end of lunch break. "Let's go" Emma said, pulling Timmy, who was lost in thoughts, along.

As they walked back to class, Timmy felt a mix of emotions. He finally felt completely relieved and unburdened, having shared his stories with Emma. His heart was filled with gratitude for her unwavering support. However, the narration of his tales had also increased his anticipation for Lythari's story, and his concern about the Guardian's secrets.

He knew the adventure was far from over.

He decided to prepone his Saturday morning calls with Grandma to today evening, she should know as well.

NINETEEN
PARTY PLANS

Two weeks flew by in a whirlwind of adventure and creativity. Lythari continued to evade Timmy's questions about his past, and Timmy, after a while, stopped asking because he felt if he pushed too much Lythari might change his mind about the meeting with Timmy's parents.

On a positive note, Timmy's school life flourished. His artwork garnered recognition in the school exhibition. His stories won praise from his English teacher. He had finally learnt to strike a balance between his imagination and his academics, between creativity and recognition.

Emma remained his closest confidante. Together, they discussed Lythari's elusive nature.

"Maybe he's protecting himself" Emma would suggest.

"Or hiding something big" Timmy would counter.

But despite Lythari's secrecy, Timmy's trust in him deepened. Their bond grew stronger with each passing day.

Lythari's deflections, though, became subtler every time Timmy asked him about when he was planning to arrange the meeting.

"A story for another time, Timmy."

"Patience, young adventurer."

"The path ahead requires focus."

Timmy began to doubt if Lythari would ever reveal his secrets, but Emma's encouragement kept his curiosity alive.

"Lythari will open up when the time is right, Timmy. Don't worry."

But as the days turned into weeks and Lythari seemed to forget about his promise, Timmy's patience began to falter. He wondered if Lythari would ever share the truth with him, if he even considered Timmy understanding enough to talk about his past with him.

Timmy's eleventh birthday was just round the corner, and excitement filled the air. During recess, Emma, Max, Olivia and Timmy huddled together to plan the perfect celebration.

"Party plans!" Emma exclaimed, fists in air, and Timmy grinned shyly, but eager to start brainstorming.

They decided on a cosy, intimate gathering at Timmy's house, with a guest list comprising close friends and family. The menu would feature Timmy's favourite pizza and cake, accompanied by balloons, streamers, and a photo booth for decorations. For entertainment, they opted for board games, treasure hunt and karaoke.

While planning the details, Emma suggested a themed party.

Immediately, Olivia chimed in, "How about a theme called 'Magical Adventures'? You know, Timmy would love that. Won't you, Timmy?"

Timmy's eyes sparkled at the idea. Emma scribbled notes, envisioning Lythari-inspired decorations, a 'Lost City of Gold' cake, and encouraging guests to wear costumes. Max and Olivia initially questioned them what all of this was about, then they figured it was probably some inside joke between the two best friends, and stopped asking.

Timmy's face lit up at the prospect of inviting Lythari, which Emma secretly whispered into his ear, asking, "Do you think he'll come?" Timmy nodded confidently, knowing that Lythari would make an appearance. How could he not? It was his dear friend's birthday, after all.

With plans unfolding, Timmy's anticipation grew, knowing this birthday party would be unforgettable – a celebration of friendship, adventure, and magic.

On Friday night, Emma and her parents joined the Tints' family for dinner, as they enjoyed a warm evening together. Mrs Tint had prepared a delicious dinner, and it's sweet aroma filled the entire house. What more could a person want in life, Timmy thought, if they had roasted chicken with herbs and lemon, garlic and butter mashed potatoes, steamed broccoli with a sprinkle of cheese, freshly baked dinner rolls, and green salad with assorted dressings for dinner.

Emma complimented Mrs Tint on the spread at the dinner table.

"Your cooking is amazing, 'Mrs Timmy's mummy'!" she had been calling her by this adorable name since she was all of four and none of them wanted to change that.

Mr and Mrs Mathews agreed smiling, nodding their heads as they savoured the dishes.

"Thanks, Emma darling! I'm glad you're enjoying it."

After dinner, Mr Tint poured everyone glasses of fresh lemonade. The parents engaged in a conversation about their children's school, weekend plans, and eventually Timmy's birthday party.

"I don't think we need to mention it separately every year" said Mr Tint to Mr and Mrs Mathews, "but your daughter is very much invited!"

"Oh, we made that part out, thank you very much" came the response, and the drawing room filled with warm, hearty laughter.

After the conversations were over and Mrs Tint had washed up the dishes, Mr and Mrs Mathews decided to leave. Since it was getting pretty late, they wanted to take Emma along, but Emma insisted that she had stayed till much later at Timmy's house before, and since their houses were only two streets apart, her parents agreed.

Once they had left, Timmy looked at Emma, who nodded knowingly. He cleared his throat, and said, "Mummy, Daddy, I wanted to discuss my birthday plans with you."

Mrs Tint nudged her husband on the chest, and he looked away from the television screen which he had just switched on. He muted the sound, and looked at Timmy. "Go ahead, son" he said.

"Yes, sweetie. Tell us what you and Emma have thought" Mrs Tint encouraged.

Timmy shared his ideas. All he wanted was a cosy party at home with close family members and friends. The theme would be 'Magical Adventures', and the decorations would be Lythari-inspired.

His parents listened attentively. When he was done, Mr Tint clapped in excitement. "We love it!!" he exclaimed.

"It's a great idea, honey. Can we help with anything?" Mrs Tint asked, happy seeing that her son was finally becoming active in his own life.

Timmy grinned.

"Just your input and permission."

"Well then, you have it!" they chimed in unison.

Mr Tint suggested inviting Timmy's Grandma ahead. She would obviously come on his birthday like every year, without question, but inviting her beforehand would engage them in conversations about Lythari. They didn't know Timmy had already spoken to her on phone on the subject. Timmy and grandma shared many secrets which were safe from the elders.

"We should call her! What do you think, Timmy?"

Timmy's face lit up. "Yes, of course!" he leaped in joy.

Grandma answered on the first ring. "Hello, dear. How are you?" she said in a slow, kind voice.

"I'm fine, Grandma" said Timmy, then proceeded to explain the party plans.

Grandma's enthusiasm echoed through the phone. "I wouldn't miss it!" she said cheerfully.

The family cheered. With Grandma on board, the party planning gained momentum.

Emma beamed. "This is going to be epic!" she said pressing her eyes shut and popping her mouth.

Timmy's heart swelled with joy. His birthday party would unite all the people he loved in the world, and beyond.

His mind went to Lythari. How great would it be to be wished happy birthday by the Guardian, who also happened to be his closest friend, he thought.

Over the next three days, Timmy and Emma crafted handmade invitations after school and during recess. They carefully selected a small group of close friends to share Timmy's special day. Besides max and Olivia, there was Samantha, the class president, Ben, the math whiz, and Alex, the sports enthusiast.

As they received the invitations, their reactions were priceless.

Samantha's eyes widened. "A Magical Adventures themed party? I'm so in!"

"I love the map design inside the invite!" said Ben, looking at the intricate map Timmy had drawn of all the places he had journeyed to with Lythari. Only he and Emma knew what it stood for.

Alex grinned. "Count me in for the games and food! I'll also bring my gaming console for some friendly competitions."

All of them promised to come dressed in their best adventure-inspired attire.

As Timmy and Emma collected enthusiastic RSVPs, Timmy's excitement grew. He knew that his small but lively friends' group would make his birthday unforgettable.

TWENTY
DRAGON'S DEN

In the midst of all this planning, Timmy did not forget to spend time with Lythari. He remembered how hurt his magical friend was last time when he had been busy with the Art Camp, and did not want him to feel left out this time. They continued going on adventures together. In Timmy's dreams, he and Lythari soared through skies, leaving the familiar earthly landscapes behind.

On one such night, Lythari visited his friend a little earlier than usual, since Timmy had just fallen asleep.

"Tonight, Timmy, we venture to ancient China" the Guardian announced. "The realm of the Great Dragons."

Timmy mounted up on his back, and off they went.

As they descended onto the rolling hills of China's countryside, they were enveloped by a picturesque landscape. Endless fields of emerald green rice paddies stretched towards the horizon, with misty mountains rising in the distance. Ancient villages nestled among the hills, their traditional tile-roofed houses and curling smoke from chimneys creating a sense of timeless tranquillity. Farmers tended to their crops, while water buffalo lazily grazed in the nearby fields.

A serene lake shimmered in the distance, reflecting – and Timmy couldn't believe what he saw – majestic dragons of different colours as they landed gracefully amidst this tranquil scene. Lotus bloomed around the lake's edges, their delicate petals swaying gently in the breeze. The air was filled with the sweet scent of jasmine and cherry blossoms, accompanied by the soothing sounds of chirping cicadas and soft chimes from hidden temples.

Longwei, an emerald green dragon and the largest there, spoke as Timmy dismounted from Lythari's back.

"Welcome, Lythari and young Timmy. Welcome to our homeland" he said, his voice rough but welcoming.

Lythari smiled, his eyes shining with knowledge.

How many ever times this happened, Timmy could never really get used to be so known at the magical verse. He was surprised at hearing his name.

"China's countryside holds secrets of ancient magic and timeless wisdom, and tonight, we will go discovering one of those. Tonight's adventure is the quest for the Dragon's Pearl" he informed Timmy, as they prepared to embark.

The Great Dragons of China were majestic creatures, their physical appearance a testament to their ancient power and wisdom. Longwei, being the largest dragon, stood proudly, his jade green scales glistening in the sunlight and shimmering with intricate patterns. These patterns -Timmy recalled, from their kitchen, resembled the finest Chinese ceramics, with delicate swirls and curls that seemed to dance across the dragon's body. His crimson eyes, pools of deep wisdom, shone like polished amber, and his magnificent wings, strong and broad, stretched wide, their membranous skin translucent and etched with veins of gold. When he moved, his wings rippled and flowed like silk, sending gentle breezes through the air. His majestic head, adorned with a slender horn, held high, exuded a quiet confidence and authority. A flowing mane, like golden silk, cascaded down his neck, framing his noble face.

The other dragons, equally impressive, displayed their unique characteristics. Maroon scales glowed on the fiery dragon, Huo, while golden yellow scales shone brightly on the radiant dragon, Jin.

Each dragon's claws, sharp and curved, gleamed like polished jade, and their powerful tails swished with gentle strength, balancing their movements. When they moved, their scales shimmered and glowed, reflecting the colours of the Chinese landscape – Timmy recalled from his mythology books – green for growth, red for energy, yellow for wisdom, and gold for prosperity.

Their physical presence seemed to embody the very essence of China's ancient magic and timeless wisdom. Timmy felt humbled and awestruck, standing alongside these magnificent creatures, his heart filled with wonder and reverence.

The dragons' wise eyes regarded Timmy and Lythari.

"We seek the legendary Dragon's Pearl," Lythari informed them. "The hidden treasure within the Great Wall."

The dragons nodded their humongous heads understandingly.

"Ride with us" Longwei invited.

Timmy settled onto Longwei's back. Lythari climbed up on Jin's. This was a new kind of experience for Timmy, since he had only ever ridden on Lythari's back before. With a mighty roar, the dragons took flight.

They soared above the Great Wall, watchtowers and battlements whizzing by. Through valleys and mountains, villages and waterfalls, the dragons flew, their wings beating in unison.

As they flew, Lythari shared tales of China's ancient magic with Timmy. He told him about the dragons' connection to the land and their role as the Guardians, to which Timmy shouted "Just like you" to Lythari, who smiled back.

Timmy listened to the tales, entranced.

As the sun began to set and golden light danced across the landscape, Longwei and Jin led them to a hidden chamber within the Great Wall's ancient stones.

A glowing pearl rested on a pedestal. The Dragon's Pearl.

Longwei nudged Timmy. "Claim the pearl" he whispered.

Timmy looked at Lythari, and saw him smiling. Lythari nodded, and raised his wings in a gesture of wishing him luck.

But as soon as Timmy reached for the Dragon's Pearl, an unseen force field repelled him. The air thickened, like an electric charge, and the pearl began to glow with an intense, pulsing light.

"Respect the ancient trials" Longwei's voice echoed.

"Prove your worth" echoed Jin's.

The chamber transformed into a labyrinth, where shadows danced and illusions swirled.

Timmy stumbled. He felt disoriented.

But just then, Lythari's words came whispering into his ears from somewhere. "Focus on the pearl's heartbeat. Listen to its rhythm."

Timmy concentrated, regaining faith in himself. The pearl's pulse synchronized with his own.

As he concentrated deeper. He saw a hidden doorway materialize in front of him. The doorway was guarded by armour-clad warriors.

Lythari's voice echoed through the walls, "The key is not to fight but to tire them out. But keep your energy"

Timmy nodded determinedly. On seeing him, the warriors came running down, their spectral swords clashing.

Timmy dodged, dunked and weaved them, as Lythari's wisdom guided his movements.

"Harmony, not strength."

"Balance, not force."

Timmy followed these instructions, and eventually, the warriors tired out and vanished.

In place of the doorway, now a vortex swirled.

The moment Timmy stepped forward, a blinding light from the pearl enveloped him, and invisible threads bound him, testing his resolve.

A snake-like voice whispered in a hiss, "Tell me, young Timmy, what is it that your heart truly wants? Is it wisdom? Or is it power?"

Timmy focused on his heart.

"I seek wisdom. To protect and to serve" he said in a calm voice.

Immediately, the threads around his arms loosened, and Timmy unbound himself. He noticed that the pearl's glow had softened.

"Trial passed," Longwei's voice resonated. "You can claim the Dragon's Pearl."

With reverence, Timmy caught the pearl, and enclosed it within his palm. He felt its warmth spread and its wisdom slowly flood his mind.

Once he got hold of the pearl, the chamber dissolved. Timmy walked outside. The Great Dragons, along with Lythari, awaited him outside. Timmy saw that the night had passed, and it was dawn now. The sun had risen, and it was a new day.

A surge of wisdom, courage and confidence flowed through Timmy.

"Timmy, son of adventure, you have earned the Dragon's Pearl," Longwei roared. "Your heart holds the spirit of exploration."

As abruptly as the dream had begun, it now started to fade. The dragons' proud roars as they faced the sky and welcomed Timmy were the last things Timmy saw and heard, before he woke up.

His excitement bubbled over as he returned to his bedroom, still reeling from their adventure in ancient China. Lythari stood by him, looking proud.

"It was a thrilling adventure, Lythari!" he said, then before the latter could respond, he exclaimed, "You must come to my birthday party. The tales we would tell everybody!" barely able to contain his enthusiasm.

Lythari's eyes clouded with concern.

"I'm afraid that won't be possible, dear friend" Lythari said, his voice low and measured.

"What? Why not?" Timmy asked, persistence creeping into his tone. "It's my birthday, the best day of the year! And you are my best friend! You have to be there."

Lythari's gaze softened, his expression a mixture of understanding and regret.

"Timmy, my existence must remain secret" Lythari explained. "If others were to discover my presence, it could put you and those you care about in danger. As it is, you've already told them about me. And I don't blame you for that. You did the right thing by choosing not to lie. But now it's time for me to do the right thing, which is to protect you. If I don't appear at your party, they probably would forget about the whole thing, and think I was a figment of your imagination. Let it be that way, Timmy."

"But it's just one day!" Timmy pleaded. "Just a few hours! Only Mummy, Daddy, Granny and Emma will be there to greet you. I promise I won't let the others near you, I've talked about it with my parents. But if, at all, you want to meet my friends, I can introduce Max and Olivia to you, too. They are just as nice, and they would understand. We can all play games together. This is an adventure too, a quest outside our dreams, like that night we had corndogs by the riverside"

"And almost made the newspaper headlines" Lythari said flatly, " No , I won't risk that for you again"

Lythari's eyes searched Timmy's, seeking to convey the gravity of the situation. He probably couldn't express in words!

"Timmy, you don't understand," Lythari said gently. "My presence will attract unwanted attention. There are those who will seek to exploit my powers, and others who will fear what they don't understand. They will make fun of me, insult me in the worst possible ways, because my existence is beyond their comprehension."

Timmy's face fell, but his resolve remained unshaken.

"Please, Lythari?" Timmy asked, his voice barely above a whisper. "This is the only time I'm insisting you to this extent. Because it's the most important day of my life, and you the most important friend. Can you make it? Just this once? For me?"

Timmy knew, the reason was just not this, he recalled the overheard conversation in his mind and wondered if Lythari remembered his life before he became magical. He was convinced either Lythari doesn't remember any of it or he had some reason to hide. Some hurt like his parents had been hiding for six years now.

Lythari hesitated, his expression torn.

"I will think on it," he said finally in a voice laced with reluctance. "But promise me, dear friend, you will not speak of me to anyone anymore."

Timmy nodded eagerly, his heart racing with hope.

"I promise! I won't tell anyone else."

" But you also promise to keep your promises , you said there'll be two quests, one to the magical realm and one diving in your past! That never came. And you promised to meet my parents too..."

" All in good time Timmy, I'll keep my promises, have faith dear friend."

Lythari's gaze lingered on Timmy's, searching for any sign of deception. "Remember, Timmy," he warned, "Secrecy is crucial. I don't care about my safety, but yours depends on it as well."

And with that, he vanished into the shadows, leaving Timmy alone and wondering.

TWENTY-ONE
BIRTHDAY

Saturday morning dawned bright and sunny, filled with excitement and anticipation. Grandma had already arrived to help with the birthday preparations. Timmy's eyes sparkled with joy as the doorbell rang and he rushed to get her luggage.

"Grandma's here!" Timmy exclaimed, hugging her tightly.

Mr and Mrs Tint were overjoyed to see the cheerful old lady of seventy, still going strong, and Timmy so happy and lively.

"Let me get Grandma's coat. You guys rush to the market!" Mrs Tint said, addressing Timmy and his father.

The two of them set off for the market, eager to begin their shopping spree. The market bustled with activity, colourful stalls overflowing with fresh produce, vibrant flowers, and an array of decorations.

Timmy's eyes widened as they walked through the stalls.

"Look, Daddy! Balloons! And streamers!"

Mr Tint chuckled.

"Alright, son. Let's get everything we need."

First, they went to the bakery. As soon as they entered, Timmy's face lit up. "Cakes!" he squealed.

The baker, Mrs Lee, greeted them warmly.

"Happy birthday in advance, Timmy! Which cake would you like?"

Timmy scanned the display case. "That one!" he pointed.

A magnificent cake shaped like a paw with two wings caught his eye. The paw was adorned with intricate details, and the wings sparkled with edible glitter.

"Amazing choice!" Mrs Lee encouraged.

After she was done carving out Timmy's name on the cake, she handed them the packet along with candles and a knife. Timmy beamed. He was very happy with his choice of the cake.

Next, they visited the decoration stalls, selecting vibrant colours and themes that matched the walls of Timmy's bedroom and the drawing room, and also his creative, adventurous personality. He also chose beautiful flowers to adorn the tables.

As they continued shopping, Timmy's excitement grew.

"This is going to be the best birthday so far!" he squealed

Once they were done, Timmy and his father headed home, laden with bags and bundles.

Time to transform the house into a magical celebration zone, Timmy thought.

Tomorrow, his special day would unfold. A day filled with laughter, love, and adventure.

Sunday morning with all its joy, love and merrymaking. Timmy's heart filled with warmth and gratitude as he woke up to a chorus of "Happy Birthday" sung by his parents and Grandma, accompanied by tight hugs and loving cuddles.

"Happy birthday, sweetie!" his mother gave him a big kiss on the cheek.

"May this year be the best year of your life" his father said, patting the back of his neck.

"Daddy, you say that every year" Timmy teased, and all of them laughed.

Grandma showered him with kisses all over his face.

"Today's my special boy's special day!" she exclaimed.

As he sat up in bed, Mrs Tint showed him her phone. Numerous "Happy birthday to dear Timmy" messages flooded the screen, as friends and family sent warm wishes for him.

Timmy smiled wide, feeling loved.

After a quick breakfast, he joined his parents in decorating the house. Streamers and balloons transformed the living room into a vibrant party zone.

"Where should we hang the banner?" asked Mr Tint.

"Above the lunch table?" Timmy suggested.

"Perfect!" Grandma shouted from the kitchen.

As they worked, the aroma of delicious food wafted from the kitchen. Mrs Tint was busy preparing a feast, and Grandma was giving her a helping hand.

"Can I help?" Timmy offered.

"Not yet, dear. Maybe next year?" said Grandma, and winked at her daughter-in-law.

"Get ready for the party, Timmy," called his father, "Your friends will arrive soon."

Timmy rushed to wash up and change into his new birthday outfit – a bright blue shirt with a golden dragon emblem. His favourite adventure-themed attire.

Excitement built up inside him.

Would his friends like the party?

Would Lythari surprise him?

His mind reeled with thoughts. "Whatever happens," he said to himself, "Today's going to be unforgettable!"

As he finished getting ready, the doorbell rang.

"First guests are here!" his father announced from downstairs.

Timmy rushed to get the door. His friends from school ran inside, Emma, Max and Olivia leading the way. Timmy hugged them as they all wished him. Then, before closing the door, he took a look outside. His mind wandered to the one guest he secretly hoped would attend – Lythari. Will Lythari come? he thought. Or did he change his mind? He said he'd think about it. Was that just to evade the question?

Timmy's excitement about the party was tinged with a hint of uncertainty. He had promised Lythari that he would understand his situation, but his silly heart longed to share this special day with his mysterious friend.

As he mingled with his guests, his eyes occasionally drifted toward the door, hoping to catch a glimpse of Lythari's unmistakable presence. Maybe he'll surprise me, Timmy comforted himself.

The morning was almost over, and it would soon be the time for lunch, but Lythari remained absent.

Timmy tried to focus on the laughter and joy surrounding him. The games at the party that Alex had brought along were an absolute blast. His friends eagerly gathered around the table, ready to dive into the fun.

First up was 'Treasure Hunt Adventure' designed by Timmy's father. Clues were hidden around the house, leading the kids on an exciting journey.

"Find the hidden treasure!" Mr Tint announced, and let out a whistle.

The kids scattered, searching high and low.

Laughter echoed, and shouts of excitement filled the air.

The kids collaborated in teamwork, and finally the treasure, a chest filled with gold coins (Timmy was pretty sure those were chocolate coins), was discovered.

Next, they played 'Pin the Tail on the Dragon' a birthday twist on the classic game.

Mrs Tint blindfolded each player, spun them around, and pointed them towards the giant dragon poster.

Giggles erupted as tails were pinned in hilarious places. Not one landed on the dragon's back, and most of them got stuck on its head, wing, and even belly.

Everyone laughed. Timmy loved how no one really cared who won. They were just here for the fun.

The next game they played was called 'Adventure Storytelling.' Grandma started narrating a tale.

"Once upon a time, in a land far, far away– " then pointing at Timmy, she said, "You go first, darling!"

Timmy added the next sentence, and then pointed at Emma, who then pointed at Olivia. The game continued, with them adding one sentence each, and building an epic story of dragons, magic, quests, and friendship.

Their imaginations ran wild, and together, they crafted an unforgettable adventure.

As the party continued, the games became more energetic. There were balloon pops, musical chairs, dance-offs, and laughter and joy filled the air.

Timmy beamed. "Best birthday ever!" he screamed internally.

But amidst all the fun, a tiny part of him still hoped. Hoped that Lythari would appear. He would surprise his *young adventurer*.

The cake cutting ceremony was a highly anticipated moment at Timmy's birthday party every year, because his friends looked forward to seeing what artwork or theme he had chosen. The room fell silent as Mrs Tint brought out the magnificent cake, shaped like a paw with two wings, sparkling with edible glitter. Everybody clapped at the beautiful design.

"Make a wish before blowing the candles" Emma reminded him.

Timmy closed his eyes, took a deep breath, and wished with all his heart. "Please let Lythari come. Please, please, please." He blew all the eleven candles at once.

He grasped the cake knife, and cut the first slice. The room erupted in the "Happy Birthday" song, as everyone sang and clapped in harmony.

Timmy smiled. Everybody cheered, and both Mr Tint and Max whistled at the same time.

His mother handed him the first slice. He took a bite of the moist, fluffy cake with rich, creamy frosting. "Delicious!" he exclaimed. Closing his eyes and savouring the taste, the texture and the sweetness.

His friends gathered around, eager for their turn.

Mrs Tint served the slices in different plates to them. As they savoured the cake and congratulated Timmy for having such great taste, a web of community, togetherness and love wove around them. Conversation flowed, accompanied by laughter and smiles.

Timmy's heart swelled. He was grateful for his loved ones, but he was still hoping. Hoping that Lythari would surprise him.

The cake cutting ceremony concluded. But the party continued. More games were introduced, and fun and celebrations erupted, creating for the kids some unforgettable memories.

Yet, Timmy's mind persisted. Maybe Lythari is watching from afar? Maybe he'll come later, when the time is right, Timmy tried to convince himself. But the uncertainty lingered, serving as a gentle reminder to him that some secrets were probably too precious to share, that they were better not revealed. Timmy felt a little dejected, nevertheless, he went back to playing with his friends.

The dinner bell rang, and Mrs Tint announced, "Dinner time, everyone!" The room buzzed with excitement as the kids made their way to the beautifully set dinner table. A sumptuous feast awaited, featuring Grandma's special lasagna, Timmy's mother's secret recipe chicken wings, roasted vegetables with magic sauce, golden garlic bread, pizza from the delivery as they had planned and fresh fruit salad to balance all that carb. The aroma wafting from the dishes tantalized everyone's taste buds, and Timmy's eyes widened in awe.

"Wow, Mummy! The food tastes so good! And so does your lasagna, Grandma" he exclaimed.

His friends agreed and cheered, calling it "Foodie Heaven" as they dug in. The dinner conversation flowed effortlessly, filled with laughter, stories, jokes, and friendship. As they savoured each bite, flavours danced on their taste buds, and delight filled the air. Grandma's lasagna was a hit, Mrs Tint's chicken wings disappeared quickly, and the roasted vegetables were devoured. Garlic bread was torn apart, and fresh fruit salad refreshed their palates. Dinner concluded with happy sighs, contented smiles, pizzas sliced and string cheese pulled, and full bellies.

Then, it was time for dessert, and Timmy couldn't help but wonder, would Lythari still make an appearance? Only time would tell.

For now, Timmy would cherish the love and friendship surrounding him, and hold on to his newfound hope and confidence.

Soon, dessert was over. Timmy's friends started departing one by one, and Emma, Max and Olivia lingered for a while. Eventually, Max and Olivia's parents arrived, and they gave Timmy tight hugs and cheek kisses and wished him one last time before leaving. After they had all left, and none but Timmy, his parents, Grandma, and Emma remained, they decided to gather around the table on which numerous presents were kept. Excitement sparkled in Timmy's eyes.

"Time to open your gifts!" Mrs Tint said, smiling.

The first present he opened was from Emma.

It was a board game called "A Dragon's Adventure.'

Timmy grinned. "This is everything, Emma! Thank you so much" he said, looking at his best friend.

Emma grinned back. "No problem" she said politely.

Next, he unwrapped Grandma's present. It was a beautifully crafted, leather-bound journal.

"For writing down the wild adventures that you've going on since you were five" she said. "Do you still have those dreams? I remember I used to play with you and– "

Grandma took the cue and finished " this one is to write your own adventures", she smiled kindly.

At this moment, Mr Tint let out a cough. Grandma stopped speaking, and looked at Timmy with a big smile on her face. "So, what do you think?"

Timmy hugged her. "I love it. Thank you, Grandma!"

His parents' gift to him was a stunning a state-of-the-art smart watch.

"To track your explorations" Mr Tint winked at him.

" and keep you grounded in time" Mrs Tint faked being serious but broke into a hearty smile right afterwards.

Timmy couldn't believe what was happening. He had never imagined such a day would arrive when his parents would willingly give him something in support of his dreams and adventures.

Next, he opened Max's gift. A remote-control dragon drone. Inside the packaging, there was a note that read, "Enough stories about Lythari. It's time to fly a dragon now! Love, Max."

Timmy let out a laugh, then passed the note to Emma to read. She, too, was amused. "This guy just won't change" she remarked, and they all laughed out loud.

The other gifts from his friends included a book on mysterious, mythical creatures, a puzzle of a mystical forest, a gift card to his favourite outdoor store, and a personalized adventure-themed T-shirt.

As Timmy opened each present, joy filled his heart and gratitude overflowed.

"Mummy, can you please remind me to thank everyone on the phone later tonight? For such thoughtful gifts?" he asked, addressing his mother. Mrs Tint gave him an assuring nod.

Overall, it was a wonderful birthday for Timmy. Love and appreciation surrounded him, and he made some really unforgettable memories with his friends.

Lythari's absence still lingered in his thoughts, but for now, Timmy basked in happiness.

After a while, Grandma spotted Timmy and Emma sitting at the table, talking to each other. They were smiling, but Grandma could make out some serious undertones. Her keen eyes noticed a hint of distraction in Timmy's smile, which appeared to her forced in order to avoid suspicion.

"Hello sweeties, what are you smiling and talking about?" Grandma asked in her slow, kind voice.

Hearing her, they immediately stopped talking, and Emma stood up, smiling politely at Grandma.

"Alright, Timmy. I better go now, it's pretty late already" she said, looking at Timmy with a soft expression on her face. "And remember, if you want to talk about anything, I'm here, okay?" she added , her voice concerned.

Timmy nodded. "Thanks, Emma," he said, then whispered to her, "And I'm sorry you waited so long for nothing."

Emma waved off his apology, bid goodbye to Grandma and Mr and Mrs Tint, and left.

"What was that all about?" Grandma asked, once she was gone.

Timmy felt tired and sleepy. "It's nothing, Grandma. Just school stuff" he said, yawning.

Grandma's expression softened. "Timmy, I know you better than that. Something is wrong, tell me" she insisted.

Mr and Mrs Tint exchanged a knowing glance, then Mr Tint looked at Grandma and nodded. "I think it's the right time. We should talk about this" he said, as he looked at his son's teary eyes.

Something about their secretive glances at each other told Timmy that Grandma already knew what he and Emma were talking about. He looked into her eyes, and asked, "Talk about what, Grandma? What is Daddy talking about?" trying to sound convincingly innocent, as the eavesdropping episode was something he hadn't told a soul about, and he knew it was what they were referring to.

"You've told us about your dream quests with Lythari since you could talk" Grandma said.

"And very recently revealed to us that he's real" added Mrs Tint.

"Yes, I've shared everything with you three and Emma" Timmy confessed, "the only thing, I was keeping from you is my Hope that Lythari would make an appearance tonight. Remember Mummy, Daddy, that day I made a drawing of Lythari and you requested to meet him? I've been requesting him ever since. He keeps on delaying, stating one quest or the other." his voice faltered, chocking on tears, "so I decided to invite him to tonight's party, and though he didn't promise, I was really hoping he would choose today to meet you all, to prove to you that I don't lie, or hallucinate." Timmy paused, "that's what Emma was waiting for, and it's this elusiveness we were discussing right before, nothing more".

Mr Tint interjected, visibly taken aback, "we never disbelieved you Timmy, it's of course because we have full faith in you, but there's something else too" he hastily exchanged a glance with Grandma and continued, "that's why even though your principal on several occasions suggested you might be *different*, and we need to see a paediatric psychiatrist about it, we have till now not given it a serious thought."

Mrs Tint added, clearly embarrassed, "you see, you're the one with pure intentions, you're clear and pure, you haven't kept things from us..."

"But we did" Mr Tint finished her sentence.

"Well, you had to, to protect many things in this realm, just like we must protect Lythari's secret, now that five people already know" Grandma paused ". But I knew Lythari even before you started telling me your dream adventures over our Saturday morning calls, even before your father mentioned him to me. In fact, I knew him even before *any of you* knew him" said Grandma.

Timmy's eyes widened. "How did you know?" he asked. He could now link all these information to the conversation he had overheard between his parents. But he could sense there was even more to it. He was curious to know everything about his best friend of the magic realm, his Guardian Angel.

"You know the other day, when you came to our bedroom and said you wanted to talk about your dreams? That wasn't the first time we got to know about them. We've been noticing changes in you, Timmy, and Daddy and I suspected something more to these dreams than merely going on adventures, like you used to say" his mother explained.

"Your imagination, your curiosity... it's as if you're connecting with something deeper," added his father introspectively. " the name Lythari was familiar to us , but we thought, it's just a name you might have picked up from a book and stayed with you in your imagination, pure coincidence."

Tears welled up in his mother's eyes. "But then you drew him and we knew...It's true that we've been worried about you, in the beginning, for a long time, we thought you may be losing touch with reality, too engrossed in your imagination, but we are also very proud of you, darling," she said, her voice breaking.

"Proud?" Timmy asked, confused. He felt he would start crying at any moment, and tried to hold his tears back.

"Yes, proud" his father emphasized.

"Because you're experiencing something extraordinary, Timmy," said Grandma. "Something that not many people understand."

" And its helping you grow, beyond just your marvellous imagination and creativity, its helping you grow to be an empathetic, understanding, kind and gentle human with pure intentions, values and purpose" Mr Tint added.

"You understand?" Timmy choked, "you believe?" He couldn't complete the sentence.

" Well, that's how you've given us the impression Timmy" his mother tried to cheer him up, wiping his tears , " it's your birthday, Timmy, don't cry, it breaks my heart".

The room fell silent. Timmy felt at that moment a thousand emotions were swirling between them.

After a momentary pause, Grandma placed her hand on Timmy's and asked, her voice barely above a whisper, "Lythari is real, isn't he?

He appears to you even outside of your dreams?" she asked gently. " You've told me before on phone, but remind me dear, for my ageing memory isn't very fresh".

Timmy recalled the night Lythari had come to visit him, how they had sat on the roof talking for hours, and then how they had gone on a tour round the city, the delicious corndogs, the Flying Boy incident...

Tears streamed down his face. He nodded.

"I thought I was going crazy."

Grandma hugged him tightly. "You're not crazy, dear. You're special."

At these words, Timmy looked up. Lythari used to tell him the same.

"We love you, Timmy" said his parents, as they joined the hug.

Timmy closed his eyes, not wanting to let go. In that moment, he not only felt loved but also understood and accepted.

After they had let go, Timmy looked at Grandma. "So, tell me about Lythari, you said you knew him even before any of us" he said curiously. Grandma's eyes sparkled with nostalgia.

"Timmy, when you were four years old, you lived with me for a few months," she began. "You were a curious toddler, always exploring. Your mom was pregnant and very very unwell, so I was given the joyous task to take care of you. But I had my beach stall to manage by daytime and old age, couldn't keep up with all the toddler energy, as much fun as it was" she confessed, "And to keep you company, I got a playful puppy. A fluffy little happy energetic Husky puppy" She paused. "His name was Lythari" she revealed.

Timmy was overcome with surprise and shock as Grandma continued her story. She told him that a toddler Timmy and Lythari were inseparable, and they often used to have small adventures together, like chasing butterflies in the garden and searching for berries in the ground. They would play games with each other, like hide-and-seek behind the curtains, fetch-the-ball, and would always cuddle on the couch, where Lythari would try to snatch the newspaper from Grandpa's hands.

They would often take their adventures to the beach, digging in sand, building sand hills band playing with corals and shells that washed ashore.

As Lythari learned tricks, Timmy learned empathy. Together, they planned to discover the world.

"But," said Grandma, and her voice broke, "God had other plans. When everything was going well, fate intervened. Your Mummy lost the baby"

Grief consumed them. Timmy let his fears flow as he got to know that in their vulnerable state, they blamed Lythari. They called him a misfortune, a bearer of bad luck.

Grandma's voice trembled. "Your Daddy took you away asked me to give Lythari away." Tears welled up in her eyes. "But I couldn't bear to part with him," Grandma confessed. "Your father, my son, and your mother, the daughter by law and heart were struggling, struggling with unthinkable immense grief over the lost baby, your mother's vulnerable health, deteriorating mental health and the pressure to keep things together so it didn't affect you" she paused. " I didn't want to trouble them further and cooked up a story about a loving, welcoming, well equipped family who were eager to have him."

This information was new not only for Timmy but his parents as well, the weight grandma must have been bearing all these years to keep such a big secret!

Grandma continued that she planned to keep raising the pup till things at the Tint household settled back to normal, which she was convinced would happen pretty fast, and then would reunite the two little inseparable friends and reveal everything. She strongly believed Lythari's presence would speed up healing their broken hearts.

But not for long. Timmy's absence broke the poor dog's heart. He was devastated. He grew despondent, and wandered off on his own one day, escaping notice.

"Then, tragedy struck," said Grandma, weeping. "That evening, our neighbours came running to us, informing that Lythari had been hit by a car while crossing the road, and was badly wounded. We rushed to the streets and took him to the vets. They fought to save him, but it was too late. Lythari's lively eyes had closed forever."

Grandma's voice cracked. "I couldn't tell you, Timmy. I couldn't tell anyone. I'm sorry." "I missed him terribly," she continued, "and always thought about the good times we spent together. Then, last week, your parents called, and your Daddy asked me if I knew something about your dreams. Because they didn't know it was your and my secret. That's when I told him all of this. I think Lythari has come back to you, Timmy."

Tears streamed down Timmy's face. He didn't even notice that Grandma, Mummy and Daddy had a truce behind his back, which at other times would have mattered a lot.

They all hugged and let the Tears flow.

Lythari, his childhood companion, his soul buddy.

Lost.

Found.

Lost again...

TWENTY-TWO
LUMO

They sat there for a long, long time, hugging each other and crying for Lythari. The clock struck eleven. They stood up, rubbing their eyes, and decided to go to bed. Timmy would sleep with Grandma tonight, as they do every time grandma came over.

As they prepared to leave the drawing room, a sudden pop sounded from the kitchen, shattering the emotional intensity in the room. Everyone started, and turned to look. Mr Tint let out a gasp, Mrs Tint a scream, and Grandma just stood there with her eyes and jaw wide opened, as they saw a magnificent white dog standing tall at the kitchen door, its eyes shining with an otherworldly light.

Lythari!

The magical creature stood there, with wings shimmering like stardust spread wide and a gentle smile etched on his face.

Timmy had never run faster in his life. He rushed towards his friend, his heart racing with joy and wonder. "Lythari! You came!" he exclaimed, his voice trembling slightly.

Lythari approached the kitchen table, his wings fluttering softly, and took out a small, shimmering gift box from under them, He placed it on the table. The box bore Timmy's name, inscribed in glittering letters. He smiled at Timmy.

"Lythari," Mrs Tint repeated, stunned. "But...but you were..." Her voice trailed off.

Grandma stepped forward, tears still streaming down her face. "Lythari, my dear boy, you've come back."

Lythari's gaze met Grandma's, and a deep understanding passed between them.

"You kept my memory alive" he said, his voice loud and echoing. "I thank you for that."

"I have come to reveal my story to you," he continued. "As promised," he looked at Timmy and winked. "Why are all your faces teary and snotty?" he joked, instantly uplifting the energy of the room , " cheer up, its Timmy's birthday, and I'm here too" he smiled broadly.

Timmy smiled. Lythari began his tale. He talked about how much he enjoyed playing and spending time with little Timmy, and how sad he was when his only friend in this world left. Then, he looked at Grandma and said, "I too was small and inexperienced Granny, had I known you planned to reunite us soon, thinking back now, running away was stupid, so so stupid. What was I thinking! I thought I could run all the way and reach Timmy."

For the first time, Grandma looked shocked and hurt.

" It wasn't the drivers fault Granny, I was too small to understand the roads and I was running frantically , haphazardly and in the most confusing manner, searching for Timmy everywhere. It was no one's fault. None of you or even the driver should feel guilty, it was meant to happen that day."

"I was more than just a dog. I was a Guardian, a companion, a bridge between worlds."

His eyes locked into Timmy's.

"You see, Timmy, I did leave this world, but I never really forgot you. All those adventures that we'd had together, my mind kept reeling with their memories. And so, I came back to you. In your dreams. Our bond remained unbroken."

" But it came with a cost for me. I could never truly belong to any one realm. While here I long for the magic verse and while there I long for you. Not that I regret any single moment of this sweet confusion."

" My ancestors have been guiding me, so I can find solace and stability and this must come to a closure".

Timmy's heart overflowed with emotions. He opened his arms wide, and approached his dear friend, his truest companion.

Lythari's wings enveloped Timmy in a warm, comforting embrace. "I came to guide you," Lythari said, "to help you unlock your true potential." "And I think I did a pretty good job" he teased, and winked again.

Timmy laugh-cried. As they held each other, the room filled with a radiant light, illuminating the depths of their connection. In that embrace, revelations unfolded to Timmy. Lythari's presence in his dreams, the meanings hidden deep within the dreams, and their shared destiny.

Timmy's parents and Grandma stood there, smiling, while tears streamed down their faces. They realised the magnitude of Lythari's role in their lives. *A magical creature, a loyal companion, and a symbol of hope.*

Revelations continued unfolding:

Lythari's presence in Timmy's dreams.

The hidden meanings, lessons.

Their shared Destiny.

Lythari patted Timmy on his back, and said, "Timmy, what I'm about to say now might make you a bit sad. But I want you to know that it's for your own good, and the good of your loved ones." Timmy prepared himself. The Angel's words came crashing down like waves on him, piercing Timmy's heart like a dagger. But deep down he knew it was coming. He had been preparing himself for this day. And he knew what he was about to hear was for the best of interest for his lovely Angel friend. Letting go without guilt, regret or grief for too long was another lesson he had to learn today. Letting go was a part of growing up.

"The magical realm does not support our connection, dear friend," Lythari explained, his voice laced with sorrow. "It's against their laws of the cosmos. Once you leave this world, willingly or unwillingly, you can't come back. But I did, and now I have to go."

Timmy's face crumpled. How much ever he could have prepared himself, He still felt like someone had hit him multiple times and he had nothing to defend himself with.

Lythari's wings drooped.

"I'll have to stop visiting soon, Timmy."

Timmy couldn't hold back his tears any longer. He burst into tears. Mrs Tint and Grandma wept, and Mr Tint, too, rubbed his eyes.

"The laws of the realm I come from are clear. We aren't supposed to have any attachments to mortals" said the Angel, his tone hurting but resolute.

Timmy felt as if his world had come crumbling down. He clung to Lythari. But he understood. He couldn't speak, lest his tears get misinterpreted as him not wanting to let go of Lythari.

The Angel understood the unspoken.

Lythari's wings enveloped Timmy tighter.

"My dear Timmy," he said into his ears in a timid voice. "I'll always be there with you. In your heart. In your creations. In your thoughts."

"But you won't visit me anymore? I won't be able to see you again?" Timmy asked, sobbing into Lythari's wings. His resolution to not pull him back shattered. His hope and familiarity, bonding and friendship took over.

Lythari shook his head. "I'm afraid that won't be possible any more, my friend. Our time together was limited. But I want to know from the deepest corner of your heart, that every single moment I have spent with you in the last five years, has been, to me, the most precious of all memories. And so have you, Timmy."

Timmy couldn't stop his tears from flowing. "Likewise, Lythari. Likewise."

As Lythari prepared to depart, the whole family gathered around him for one last hug, for one last whisper.

"Remember, Timmy," Lythari said. "Our bond shall always remain unbroken." Then he pointed at the kitchen table.

Timmy rubbed his tears off his eyes and face, and looked at the box on the table. It had two small holes on its surface, and he noticed that something inside it was moving. He quickly opened the box, and a small puppy, fluffy and innocent, looked up at Timmy, its round, adorable eyes shining like Lythari's.

"A gift," Lythari's voice echoed across the room. "For your birthday. Happy birthday, Timmy" he said, and at that moment, the clock stuck midnight.

"I will always be there with you"

With one final look at Timmy, and before anyone could stop him, Lythari mounted on his paws like he used to during their adventures, raised his wings in a final gesture of goodbye, and vanished into thin air, as suddenly as he had appeared.

The room was completely silent, except the slow ticking of the clock.

Grandma's tear-stained voice broke the silence. "A p– parting gift" she said between hiccups.

Timmy took the little creature carefully out of the box. Mrs Tint helped him.

The puppy looked like a miniature version of Lythari, and it yelped and snuggled into Timmy's arms.

"I'll call him Lumo" he said, looking fondly at his new buddy.

As he held Lumo, Timmy had an epiphany. He realised that through his little gift, Lythari himself lived on.

It was true that Lythari had taken piece of Timmy's heart away with him, but he had also left one here, as a symbol of their bond.

As he held the puppy's soft, tiny paws, he felt a sense of purpose surge within him, and his courage and confidence returned. Lythari had prepared Timmy for a world of adventures ahead, which he would face with his new friend by his side.

For the first time in his life, Timmy wasn't scared that Lythari was not there at his side. The Guardian's parting words echoed in Timmy's mind. *I'll always be there with you. In your heart.*

He bent down and brought his face close to the small, fluffy ears.

"I'll always take care of you, Lumo. I promise" he whispered.

Epilogue

The sun rose over the horizon, casting a warm, golden glow over the new day. Timmy's heart swelled with excitement as he anticipated the adventures awaiting him. The air was alive with the sweet scent of blooming flowers and the gentle chirping of birds, signalling the start of summer holidays in just a week.

Recess was in full swing, with children laughing and playing tag on the sun-kissed playground. Emma sat on a bench, her eyes locked onto Timmy as he approached her. His face radiated a mix of emotions – joy, sadness, and longing.

"Emma, I have so much to tell you," Timmy said, his voice trembling. "About Lythari, about Lumo... about everything."

Emma's curiosity was piqued. She had been wondering why Lythari had appeared after she left, and a part of her felt annoyed, feeling abandoned. But as Timmy began to speak, his words washed away her doubts.

"Lythari came to say goodbye," Timmy explained, his eyes welling up. "He's always been my guardian angel, watching over me. But now, it's time for me to take care of someone else – Lumo."

Emma's heart swelled as Timmy shared stories of his newfound responsibility. She saw the sincerity in his eyes, the determination to be the best guardian for Lumo.

As Timmy spoke, Emma's annoyance melted away, replaced by empathy and understanding. She realized that Lythari's timing wasn't about replacing her but about passing the torch to Timmy.

Almost overcome with emotion, Emma's eyes brimmed with tears. She had never seen Timmy so vulnerable, so open. The depth of their friendship shone brighter than ever.

"I'm so proud of you, Timmy" Emma said, her voice barely above a whisper. "You're going to be an amazing guardian for Lumo." Sounding so unlike her usual chirpy , animated dramatic self.

Timmy's face lit up with gratitude. "Thanks, Emma. That means everything coming from you."

As they hugged, Emma couldn't wait to meet Lumo. She envisioned snuggling the little pup, playing fetch, and sharing adventures with Timmy.

"Can I see Lumo soon?" Emma asked, her excitement palpable. Doing her like jiggy dance.

Timmy grinned. "Definitely! You're invited to Grandma's beach house for summer break. We'll have the best time ever!"

Emma's heart skipped a beat. The prospect of a sun-kissed vacation with Timmy, Lumo, and their friends was almost too wonderful to imagine.

Now, with the prospect of a sun-kissed vacation, he couldn't wait to create unforgettable memories with his friends. The beach house, with its creaky wooden floorboards and salty sea air, beckoned.

"Let's invite Max and Olivia too" Emma suggested, twirling and hopping as they walked towards the group.

"Hey, guys! Want to join me at Grandma's beach house for a week?" Timmy invited Max, and Olivia, his eyes sparkling with enthusiasm. They exchanged eager glances, knowing that Grandma's strict yet caring supervision would ensure their parents' approval.

As they awaited permission, Timmy's mind wandered to Lumo, his adorable new companion. He imagined the little pup's dreams, wondering if he was too small to have his own adventures in slumber. Was Lumo chasing after seagulls or playing hide-and-seek with beach crabs?

Timmy's mother outlined his new responsibilities: walks along the shore, potty training, obedience, tricks, safety, feeding, and regular vet check-ups. With each task, Timmy's sense of purpose grew.

With a resolute heart, Timmy vowed to be the best guardian for Lumo. "Lythari may have been my guardian angel," he thought, "but for Lumo, I'll be the protector. Only the best for my little friend." He envisioned lazy afternoons spent building sandcastles, Lumo by his side.

As the days passed, the group's anticipation grew. Would Max, Emma, and Olivia join the beach house escapade? Would quests await them – treasure hunts, beach volleyball tournaments, or impromptu picnics?

Or would life settle into a routine, with lazy mornings spent watching the sunrise and afternoons exploring the tide pools? The story of their summer adventures remained untold, waiting to unfold like a treasure map.

Would you join Timmy and his friends on their journey, brimming with laughter, excitement, and growth?

Let's embark on that adventure another day...

Author's Note

The seeds of this story were sown in the vibrant landscapes of my dreams. Since childhood, I've been blessed with elaborate, cinematic visions that unfold while I sleep. Some nights, I've eagerly awaited slumber, eager to escape into these Technicolor worlds.

Timmy's journey, though distinct from mine own, was born from these nocturnal adventures. Lythari, the loyal companion, may not have been part of my reality, but the essence of their bond resonated deeply.

This book is a testament to the power of dreams, where imagination knows no bounds. I hope you've enjoyed this journey, forged in the realm of the subconscious.

About Author

Rikhia Guha, fantasy author extraordinaire, finally emerges from her Kolkata hideout to gift the world The Adventures of Timmy Tint and Lythari. Armed with a gold medal in Applied Psychology (Calcutta University), Rikhia's a self-proclaimed nerd, devouring books like pizza slices or gorom bhaat e ghee (only Bengali speaking people will understand).

Inspired by ikigai, Rikhia masterfully juggles teaching psychology, running Jootique (craft manufacturing, find us on www.jootique in), painting, and writing – proving multitasking isn't just a myth!

Despite fibromyalgia's unpredictable challenges, Rikhia's inner zeal refuses to be silenced. Writing becomes therapy, fuelling her resilience through flare-ups. This debut novel is a testament to her unwavering passion.

Psychology's lessons shape her storytelling, while imagination fuels her art. Harry Potter and Doraemon remain BFFs. But let's face it: Rikhia communicates better with cats (who don't judge), puppies (who listen attentively), and babies (who don't care) than actual adults (who confuse her). No wonder she escapes into fantasy!